Snake

Melissa Stevens

This Demented Souls book, like all the Souls books, is dedicated to my dad, Wilmer 'Billy' Stephens.

When I started the series I used him as a major resource, as he'd been a police officer, machinist, gun smith, Harley rider, mechanic and so much more.

Now that he's gone, I write them in his memory.

Thanks Dad.

While I was growing up, my father had two of the best friends I've ever known of. They are the ones who taught me that family is more than just who you're related to. As I was working on *Maverick* we lost the last of them. Now that all three are gone, I miss the others nearly as much as I miss Dad.

From here on out, the Demented Souls books are dedicated to the men who taught me all about brothers by choice.

Frank Edwards (1950-2006)

Wilmer Stephens (Dad) (1952-2017)

George Claridge (1955-2022)

Contents

1.	1	1
2.	2	4
3.	3	9
4.	4	15
5.	5	19
6.	6	26
7.	7	30
8.	8	38
9.	9	45
10.	10	51
11.	11	55
12.	12	61
13.	13	65
14.	14	68

15. 15   75

16. 16   80

17. 17   86

18. 18   91

19. 19   96

20. 20   101

21. 21   105

22. 22   110

23. 23   116

24. 24   125

25. 25   132

26. 26   137

27. 27   141

28. 28   148

29. 29   151

30. 30   165

31. 31   171

32. 32   175

33. 33   182

34. 34   187

35. 35   191

36. 36   197

37. 37   203

38. 38   207

39. 39   208

40. 40   216

1

Snake stood at the front of the rows and rows of seats, all filled with people, some of which he knew, others he had never met, wondering why he'd agreed to this. Who in their right mind would stand up in front of so many people to be watched and stared at?

At least he didn't have to say or do anything but stand here, and when it was all over, he'd take his turn walking out, escorting a woman he'd met less than twenty-four hours before. He'd spend the evening with her, then he could go on his merry way, never having to worry about this again.

The speakers set up discreetly around the room began playing organ music, calling his attention back to what was going on and what he should be doing. At the familiar notes of Wagner's *Bridal Chorus* everyone in the room stood and turned toward the back of the crowd. Snake straightened his shoulders and stood, waiting. All he had to do was stand here, quietly, and wait.

Slowly, Jill, his friend's bride made her way down the aisle, one hand looped through her father's arm. Sweat trickled down the back of his neck and Snake couldn't help but wonder why he was so hot. It was only February and while the day was nice enough for an outdoor wedding it wasn't hot. At least not as long as you weren't standing in the sun.

Even then it wouldn't be bad if he wasn't wearing a leather kutte. That was probably the reason.

"Welcome to everyone who gathered with us today to celebrate the union of Jesus Martinez and Jillian Cooper in matrimony..." the voice of the officiant faded as Snake watched the faces of the women standing on the other side of his friend and his bride.

He'd met them all the night before at the rehearsal dinner at one of the nicer restaurants in town and hadn't caught more than their names, and most of them he couldn't recall now. Except for the woman he was to escort down the aisle when this was all finished and would be seated with all night. She'd caught his attention. And not just for the long dark hair curling down her back that made him want to bury his hands in and find out if it was as soft as it looked.

No, the few words he'd exchanged with Jenny had intrigued him, had made him want to sit in a corner and talk to her all night, and he hadn't talked to a woman for more than a few minutes at a time in years. He'd get their name, maybe spend a few minutes in small talk, then move on to what he was really after.

Especially during the last two years. He hadn't been able to risk the entanglement of a relationship. It would have been dangerous, not just to him, but to Maverick and the rest of the men who'd been on the mission in Texas. And entanglements like relationships with women who might say too much could be deadly when you were in a situation like that. Better to avoid them.

But that was in the past.

He'd come back to Tucson months ago and had no intention of taking another long mission, especially not an undercover one. It had been more than hard, and he was ready for something easier.

Jenny didn't seem to notice him watching her. Her attention was on the happy couple, reminding him he needed to pay attention to what was going on.

Snake forced himself to listen to the person officiating the wedding. They were talking about commitment and consideration. After only a few words of them talking about thinking about someone other than yourself, he tuned them out again.

His stomach rumbled and he hoped it would behave itself at least until the end of the ceremony. Instead of letting his attention wander around the guests, he found himself thinking about his friend. Jesus, or Gizmo as Snake knew him, had been waiting for this day for months. And now that it was here, he looked happier than Snake had seen him in years.

Then there was Jill. Snake had met Jill shortly after his return from Texas. He'd liked her, and thought she was pretty but today she was beautiful, and she seemed to glow with happiness.

He noticed as they turned to face each other, and forced himself to turn his mind to what was going on instead of his inner musings.

Snake listened as they exchanged their vows, kissed, and then turned to their guests as the officiant, someone Snake didn't recognize and likely would never see again, so he didn't pay the man much attention, pronounced them man and wife. Everyone clapped and cheered, Snake joined in, not sure if it was considered appropriate, but all the other groomsmen were, so why not? After a moment, Gizmo and Jill walked back up the aisle, then one by one the groomsmen stepped forward and held out an arm, the bridesmaid they'd been paired with would join them and they would follow the happy couple.

When Snake's turn arrived, he stepped forward, unable to keep from smiling at Jenny as he held out his arm. She smiled back as she wrapped one hand around it and together, they followed the rest of the wedding party.

Next, he knew there would be photos. He didn't know how long that would last, but he'd made the commitment and would do it, for his friends if nothing else. He hoped the food part would happen soon.

2

Jenny wasn't so sure about her partner for her brother's wedding. She'd met him the evening before, but he hadn't said more than a dozen words to her, or to anyone else from what she'd seen. Now she walked beside him as they left the ceremony, she still had to sit with him for dinner, would he be so taciturn for the entire evening?

She was determined not to let his unfriendliness keep her from having a good time. Really, how often did your only brother get married? She was going to enjoy the party while she could.

They joined the rest of the wedding party where the photographer had them posing for photos, group shots and those that would include them came first, the photographer had already let them know that she'd get these, then let them go do other things while she took couple shots, then everyone would be free to enjoy the rest of the evening.

As they all moved around and posed as instructed, she noticed that Snake, who went by a name like Snake anyway? Not that she could really expect much from a brother who preferred to be called Gizmo rather than the perfectly good Chuy he'd grown up as. She didn't understand it but most of her brother's friends went by names she didn't get.

It wasn't only the strange names that made Chuy's friends stand out, at least here. It was the white shirts and black leather vests they all wore. She was all for brotherhood and all that, but couldn't they have bypassed the vests and worn something nicer?

"Jenny!" Her brother's voice pulled her back to the present instead of her thoughts.

"Yes?" She did her best to keep her focus on the moment as she turned to find out what he needed.

"They're waiting for you to get into position," he motioned to where his bride, Jill, and all the other bridesmaids were gathered.

She hurried off, reminding herself she had a job to do here, and she needed to pay attention for a little longer, at least until they could go sit down and eat.

Later, she'd found the table she and other bridesmaids would share with the groomsmen they'd been paired up with and sat for a moment, reveling in not standing for just a few minutes, and not thinking. Or at least trying not to. She let her head fall back and her eyes close as she flexed her feet, trying to ease the ache from standing in these heels for so long.

"You okay?" an unfamiliar voice asked.

She opened her eyes to find Snake, her groomsman standing next to her, a look of concern creasing his brow.

"Yeah, I'm just enjoying being off my feet for a few minutes. I didn't have a chance to break in these heels before tonight."

He frowned and looked down at the floor where her feet were hopefully hidden beneath the table.

"Then take them off. We're through with all the formal stuff or I think we are, but you can put them back on if you need to." He looked around. "Most of the rest of tonight will be in here, and no one would mind. I'm sure you won't be the only one either." He motioned to the oversized barn like building the tables were set up inside, where the rest of the reception would be held.

Jenny frowned a moment, considering it. Would anyone mind if she kicked off her shoes and wandered around in her stockings? Her feet would get dirty, but that was no big deal, she could always wash them.

"If you're sure."

"I am." He waited while she kicked off her shoes, put them together and stood them under her chair so they wouldn't get damaged and would be out of the way.

Then he spoke again, "I came to get you because they're getting ready to serve dinner and Gizmo said they'd go through the line first and the attendants are to be right behind them. Then the rest of the guests." He held out one hand to help her up.

Surprised, she put her hand in his and let him help her to her feet, then together they went to retrieve their dinners.

They stood next to each other in the buffet line, Jenny noticed she wasn't the only bridesmaid who'd kicked off her shoes and now stood in their stocking feet. One had changed into ballet slippers instead. Why hadn't she thought of that?

"See?" Snake's voice was soft as he caught where her attention was. "I told you no one would care."

They moved forward slowly until it was their turn to pick up plates. Thankfully, flatware and napkins were already at the tables.

Jenny was surprised by how attentive Snake was. As they made it to each dish on the table, he offered some to her, serving her first before he put some on his own plate, then moving on. She got the feeling he was being polite and let him. If she'd gotten the feeling he was doing it to limit what she took or to be in any way belittling, she would have put an end to it quickly.

When they reached the end of the table, he took her plate and told her he'd meet her at the table, go ahead. Jenny frowned for a second, not sure what to do. She could of course make her way to the table, but it felt strange to do so empty handed. Instead, she went to the table where rows of filled cups sat with different drinks, picked up two cups of water and took them back to the table.

She set one cup in front of Snake and the other next to her plate and took her seat next to him. No one else had sat down yet. Jenny glanced around, wondering where the others were.

"Thank you for carrying that for me," she said as she picked up her fork and placed her napkin in her lap.

"No problem. I didn't want you to possibly stumble and spill it on yourself. That pink would show everything if you did." He shook his head and glanced around the room at the decorations. The entire room was decorated with two shades of pink, one pale, the other bright and vivid. "I'm not sure how they came up with two such opposite shades of the same color."

Jenny had thought the same thing, and wished she could have worn the other color, if she had to wear pink.

"I know, and is there anything more cliché than a wedding on Valentine's Day decorated with pink and pink?"

"They could have gone for red and pink." He caught her eye and gave her a teasing wink.

"I'm not sure but that might have been better." She felt like the barn had been hosed down with two concentrations of Pepto Bismol. Jenny liked Jill, but had wondered who had picked out the colors and decorations. She hadn't had the nerve to ask Chuy yet. He might not take the questions well.

"I guess Jill likes it or she would have fought harder for something else," Snake said between bites.

"Jill didn't pick these?"

Snake shook his head. "From what Gizmo said, she'd picked out some video game theme and her mom refused. Told her there was no way on earth, then took over. No one came out and said it, but I got the impression they were so relieved not to be doing it themselves there was little argument with whatever she planned." He lifted one shoulder and let it drop.

"I didn't know that. You must be close with Chuy."

He lifted the shoulder again in a gesture that she thought meant something different than the last time. "Closer than some. You're his sister, right?"

"I am. I don't get to see the same side of him you do, I'm sure."

"Probably." He looked over at her and watched her for a moment before speaking again. "He's your older brother, isn't he?"

She nodded, swallowed the bite she'd just taken then spoke. "How'd you know?"

"He looks older. I know it's a good idea to say that if you're trying to get on a woman's good side, but it's true. How much older is he?"

"Almost four years. Not enough that he didn't torment me when we were kids but enough that once he got to high school, I was just the annoying little sister trying to tag along when he did things."

Snake smiled.

She couldn't help noticing how much it changed his looks, not that he was bad looking either way, but the smile transformed his face so much that she wouldn't have guessed the two expressions belonged to the same face.

"That makes you what? Twenty-three, twenty-four?"

"Almost twenty-four. My birthday's in April."

He nodded but didn't say anything. Some of the other attendants joined them, finally. Jenny wondered what had taken them so long if Chuy and Jill had wanted the attendants through the line before the rest of the guests, but thought it would be rude to ask.

Conversation turned to how great the ceremony had gone and how happy Gizmo and Jill looked, Jenny sat mostly quiet as she felt a little out of place.

3

Snake noticed the way Jenny seemed to fold in on herself when the others arrived at the table. He'd never seen anything quite like it and he didn't like it. She'd been happy and outgoing, even a little sassy in her conversation with him, then the others had arrived, laughing, and talking in their own conversation and she'd withdrawn.

Not entirely. She still answered questions and put bits and pieces into the talk, but not like she had when it was just the two of them. He didn't like seeing it. Not for him, not for her. He had been enjoying their banter.

Gizmo's little sister was funny, funnier than he'd thought she might be. Partly because as much as he liked Gizmo, Snake didn't think he was particularly funny. Smart? Of course. Loyal? Certainly. A good friend? Undoubtably. But funny? Not really.

Not that Snake minded, he had other brothers who were funny, and they all had their own roles in the family that was the Demented Souls.

As this occurred to him, he couldn't help scanning the room, mentally picking out each of his brothers present, and noticing how many of them had found women in the years he'd been gone. The club that was his family had changed so much while he'd been away, but in some ways, nothing had changed.

After the meal was over, the toasts finished and the traditional dances endured, the party became more fun.

"Can I get you something to drink?" Snake asked Jenny, tilting his head toward the bar where a short line had formed but seemed to be moving quickly. He'd noticed a couple of the Demented Souls prospects were working behind the bar. He knew they'd been offered the opportunity to make some extra cash, but had told them they were invited either way and they didn't have to work. It looked like these two had taken the offer.

Jenny turned and looked at him for a moment, then looked toward the bar.

Do you know if they have frozen drinks?"

He took a closer look at the bar area, counters and the bottles around the two men who moved with what looked like efficiency in their own spaces.

"I don't think so. I don't see a blender."

She scrunched her nose as she thought. The expression did something odd low in his belly he didn't recognize.

"I'll have a margarita then, if they have the makings."

"I'm sure they do." He'd noticed several cups that looked like the citrus mixed drink so popular in the southwest. He stood and made his way to the bar. It didn't take more than a few minutes for him to reach the front of the line and place his order.

"Needed the money bad enough to work instead of party, huh?" he said to Sacket as the prospect set to fixing the drinks.

"I wouldn't say *need* exactly," Sackett said with a wry grin. "But I don't dance anyway, not if I can help it. And the money will come in handy. Besides, I've gotten pretty good behind a bar," he shrugged, "might as well make the evening go smoother for Gizmo and Jill." He set Snake's order on the counter in front of him. "Anything else?"

"Not now, but I'll be back, I'm sure. Thanks." Snake picked up the drinks as Sackett turned to the next in line and asked what they wanted.

Snake carried the drinks back to the table where Jenny still sat, head bobbing to the beat of the music while she watched the people on the dance floor.

"Here you are, and I was right. No blender." He set her drink in front of her as she twisted around. He took a sip from his own cup, a beer, at least for now, then set it on the table but didn't sit, not yet. "Want to dance?" He motioned one hand toward the dance floor.

"Not yet." She shot him a shy smile. "I need to get at least one drink in me first, maybe more. Then I'll be more willing to get up there." She picked up the cup and took a tentative sip, licked her lips then took a longer drink.

The sight of that bit of pink tongue slipping out then disappearing sent a bolt of heat and desire through him. That didn't surprise him. What surprised him was how strong it was and how he wanted to look around and make sure no one else had seen it. He liked women, but had never felt territorial about them. Odd that he should over this one he'd known less than twenty-four hours. Maybe because she was related to one of his brothers? Maybe he was being protective because of that.

"I'll be back in a bit. Let me know if you need anything."

She pulled a face that told him if she needed anything she'd see to it herself. For some odd reason, that only made him want to make sure she was taken care of even more.

Still, he turned and headed to where several of his brothers were gathered in a cluster. They all seemed to be focused on one thing, but he couldn't tell what. Not until he got closer and saw that it wasn't a what, but a who.

Ruger stood, his little girl in his arms, with several of the men around them. From this distance Snake couldn't tell if they were talking to the girl or her father, but he would know soon, since he was headed to join them. How much could a child that size understand anyway?

"She's getting so big, how old is she now?" Dumbass had one finger out to tickle her chest, the infant grabbed hold of the finger and stuck it in her mouth.

"That finger had better be clean." Ruger scowled at the kid. "And she's almost four months. I can't believe how fast she's growing. And watch out, she'll bite."

The kid shrugged. "How bad can it be. She doesn't have any teeth." Dumbass seemed content to let the kid gnaw on his finger.

Ruger gave the kid a look that said clearly the kid would learn better soon, then turned to answer another question another brother had asked. As Snake approached, it seemed the attention was split evenly between Ruger and his daughter. He joined the group, listening to what was being said, general chit chat and talk about what the club was doing, but nothing that made him glance around to see who might be listening. They all knew better than to do that.

"Ouch!" Dumbass jerked his hand back and shook it, as if that would help the sting.

Ruger shot the kid a look that said clearly that he'd been warned and got what he deserved.

"She's got quite a bite on her," Dumbass said, checking his finger, as if making sure the baby with no teeth hadn't drawn blood.

"How dare you malign such a sweet thing?" Sadist stepped up to the group and without asking reached out and lifted the baby from her father's arms. "Come see Uncle Sadist. I'll make sure everyone falls adoring at your feet, as they should." He lifted her in front of his face and talked baby talk to her for a few minutes, ignoring that they were in the middle of a wedding or standing amongst a group of men that handled guns with more familiarity than kids.

Snake shook his head and wondered again at all the changes to the club while he'd been gone.

"Who's going to be around the clubhouse the next couple evenings?" Ruger asked looking around the group.

"I don't have anywhere I need to be. You need someone around?" Snake said.

"We do. There's a new prospect coming in and I'm not sure when he'll arrive. I need someone to meet him, give him the tour and get him settled in. You going to be around? Can you take care of it?"

"I will and I can. What's his name?" Snake didn't have anything else he needed to be doing, as the shop where he worked would be closed the next day.

"I don't recall his given name off hand, but he goes by Boomer. I'll make sure you get more info in the morning. I'll have Krissi send it over. She's going to be covering the tech side of club business while Gizmo's gone for a couple weeks. She might not be as on top of things as he is, but Ashley is finally sleeping more than thirty minutes in a stretch, so we'll make it work."

"Is your daddy bad mouthing you, Sweetness? That's okay, you can stay with Uncle Sadist. I'll make sure everyone treats you right." Sadist continued to talk to the baby as if only the two of them existed. Well, it would seem that way if he wasn't talking to her about what was being said.

Snake frowned as he watched the large, heavily tattooed man talk to the tiny little girl in ruffles and a hair bow. The two just seemed so opposite but it was clear the club's vice president doted on that baby girl nearly as much as her father did.

Sadist moved closer to Ruger, lifted an elbow, and bumped his buddy, then when Ruger turned his attention to him, spoke. "I'm taking this little sweetheart for a dance. You want her back, you'll have to come get her."

"Nah. When she gets hungry or needs changed, you'll be happy to give her back."

Sadist didn't say anything, but shot Ruger a look as clear as words, that said that's what he thought then carried the baby out onto the dance floor. Snake heard him talking to her the whole way and couldn't help but smile at how one baby had turned some of the toughest men he knew into marshmallows.

"Where's the new guy coming from?" Havoc asked. He'd been in Texas with Snake and a couple others and had commented to Snake a couple days earlier how there were more men he didn't know in the club these days than men he knew. That wasn't quite true, but Snake understood why Havoc felt that way. A good number of the men they'd known for years were up in Wyoming, whether temporarily or for good was yet to be determined for most of them, though it looked like at least Lurch and Ghost would be staying up there.

Because of the new chapter they were adding more prospects than they usually did and voting on patching them in every six months instead of once a year like they'd done for years. He didn't know if it was a good idea or not, but he could see why they were doing it.

He listened to what was going on here for a few more minutes, then wandered away, stopping by the table to ask if Jenny needed a fresh drink then going back to the bar.

4

Jenny watched the couples dancing, noticing that occasionally a single woman would step out and dance on her own,
but couldn't bring herself to do that, not yet. She found her
attention drifting to where a group of Chuy's friends stood.
She could tell they were his friends by the leather vests they all
wore with a grinning reaper and scythe looming from behind
a motorcycle on the back.

What kind of group called themselves something as strange
as The Demented Souls? It wasn't the first time she'd wondered, but she'd never asked, so never got an answer. She also
had never spent any time with her brother's friends. She'd
known about them, but this was the first time there had been
an event where they interacted.

She wouldn't admit to anyone but herself, and maybe Chuy,
but she was curious about them. Maybe because she'd known
about them, but had never had anything to do with them
before. It took a moment before she realized that one of the
men in the group was holding a baby, and that was only when
a second one came in and lifted it from his arms.

Jenny couldn't help watching the bearded man with a weird
haircut talk to the little girl, at least that's what she assumed
from baby's pink ruffled dress, as if it was something he did
every day. After a moment, he said something to the man
who'd had the baby to begin with, then took her to the dance
floor and, staying on the edge so no one bumped into him,

began to slowly dance while still talking to the little girl. She found herself smiling as she watched them together, wondering which man was the father, the first guy or the one dancing with her now. Jenny was still watching the guy dance with the baby when Snake appeared next to her and asked if she was ready for another drink. She checked her glass and was surprised to find it almost empty.

"Please, if you don't mind."

A grin flashed across his face but was gone before she figured out what it meant. "I'll be right back."

Jenny turned her attention back to the dance floor but the guy she'd been watching was gone. She couldn't help scanning the room for him, eager for another glimpse of him with the baby. It wasn't that she was pining for a baby. She liked her sleep too much, but watching the way he'd cradled her and treated her like she was the best thing on earth, spoke to something deep inside her. She hadn't found him yet when Snake returned with her drink.

"Who is the guy with the baby?" she couldn't help asking.

"Which one?" Snake sat in his chair beside her.

"Which one?" she echoed with a frown before remembering that someone had been holding her before the guy had been dancing with her had taken her "The one dancing with her." She motioned to where he'd been on the dance floor. "It must be the second one."

"That would be Sadist." He looked around. "He's over there if you're looking for him." He motioned to the far side of the room. "But if it's the baby you're looking for she's over there with her mother, Krissi. It looks like she got hungry."

She followed his motion, not to the far side of the room but to where the baby was. It took her a moment to spot her, then realized she was only a few tables away, in the arms of a woman who appeared closer to her age, a baby blanket over her shoulder covering most of the exposed skin where she was obviously breastfeeding. Jenny looked away, not wanting to get caught watching. Her face heated and she felt like she'd been watching something intimate. Something that should be hidden. But why? Afterall, it was the most natural way to feed a baby, why should her mother be embarrassed or anyone around her? The mother, Krissi, Snake had said, didn't appear embarrassed at all. Jenny could only hope that someday, should she be in a similar situation, she was as comfortable with the people around her as this woman seemed.

There were a couple of women seated around the woman with the baby, but no men. She couldn't help but wonder if Sadist or the first guy, the one she hadn't seen, was the father. But then, who but the baby's daddy or maybe grandaddy would dance with her like that? Jenny didn't think Sadist looked old enough to be a grandfather, but what did she know?

She sat through a few more songs, watching people and sipping her drink. When they played another song with a slower beat, Snake stood.

"Can I interest you in a dance?" He held out one hand.

She stared at him, then at the hand for a moment then with one more sip, set her cup on the table, put her hand in his and stood.

"Sure." She followed him out to the dance floor.

"Tell me something about you?" Snake said as they faced each other and began to dance.

"What do you want to know?"

"I don't know. You're from around here, right?"

"Yeah. We lived in Sahuarita for a while, then moved to South Tucson when I was in middle school. I live a few blocks away now."

"Have you ever been out of the Tucson area?"

"I've been to Phoenix," she said with a shrug, not seeing why he cared.

"How about up into the mountains?"

"I've been up on A Mountain, and on Lemmon. Why?" She knew she was scowling but his questions were odd.

"Just curious about where you've been and what you've seen. I just got back into town a few months ago. I haven't seen you around the clubhouse."

"That's because Chuy discourages me from going around there."

"Discourages?"

She rolled her eyes. "He said there's no reason for me to go there. I should stay away and if I don't, he'll hear about it." Her brother was ridiculous, but she hadn't cared enough to venture over there, yet. Maybe with an incentive like Snake, she'd find a reason. That's when his words registered. "Back? Where were you?"

"Texas for a while."

"And before that? I take it you're not from around here, where are you from?"

"All over I guess, but I grew up in Northern California."

"So what's it like up there? All beaches and surfing?"

He smiled, revealing a dimple in his right cheek that she wanted to run her finger over, just to see if he'd let her but she restrained herself.

"No, that's SoCal. Northern Cali is more mountains, and forests. There are some beaches but not as much surfing because it gets pretty cold up there."

Jenny lost herself in the conversation and before she realized it, the song was over. She wasn't ready to go back to the table and sit alone again. Not that she would admit it.

"Another?" Snake asked as the opening chords of the next song played.

Joy shot through her, and heat pooled low in her belly. "Sure." Nothing would likely come of it, but she liked this guy, even if he did have an odd name.

5

S nake sat in the clubhouse, a beer in one hand and scowled at the TV. He didn't want to be here, but someone needed to be, to show the new guy around. Boomer? The name made him wonder what the guy had been doing and where he would get a name like that. Not that he thought it was odd. His own name was Snake, mostly because while he'd been in basic in Missouri, a garden snake had wandered into formation one morning, during one of the first few days of class when everyone was still getting to know each other. Several of the recruits had freaked out. A couple had run, several had frozen. And the drill sergeant had been one of the ones that had frozen. He'd been telling everyone to stay where they were, don't move and it would move on.

Snake hadn't thought much about it. He knew it was harmless, so he'd bent and picked it up, then moved it to the far side of the parade ground and let it go. After that, the sergeant hadn't bothered with his name, just called him Snake. The name had stuck. Snake hadn't minded. He'd never been fond of his given name, Garth. Too much like some country singer. As he saw it, Snake was as good as his last, Parker, though he'd been called that a lot while he was still in the service. Less so now. And he was perfectly fine with that.

The rumble of a bike pulling up in front of the clubhouse drew his attention. He didn't stir, just waited to see who came in. After a few minutes the door opened and a man stepped in,

Snake didn't recognize him, but that didn't mean too much. He looked to be in his mid-twenties, in pretty good shape, but then most of their recruits were, and still had a crew cut. The man stopped inside the door and looked around, after seeing that Snake was the only man around, headed his way.

"Are you Snake?" he asked.

"I am, and you would be?" Snake had learned a long time ago not to volunteer information. It was something that had become habit enough that he still didn't do it, not even here where he felt safe.

"I'm Boomer. I was told to meet someone here. If you're Snake, then you're the guy I'm looking for. I just got to town."

Snake looked him over, wondering how long he'd been out of the service, if he was even out yet, then took a deep breath and started on his welcome. "Can I interest you in something to drink? If you just got to town and you're on a bike, you're probably thirsty." Snake turned and looked around for the prospect who was supposed to be manning the bar but didn't see him. "Sackett!" Was it Sackett today or the other one? What was his name? Oh, that's right... "Savage!" Snake turned to Boomer. "I'm not sure which one is here, honestly. I was a little distracted when they brought me my own drink," he lifted his beer, "and I didn't notice which it was."

The new guy nodded but didn't say anything. The door to the kitchen swung open, as Savage pushed his way through and headed their way.

"What can I get you?" He looked at Snake, then Boomer, expectant.

"Boomer needs something to drink." Snake motioned to the new guy and while they talked about what was available, he checked his watch. A little after one. "He can make food too, if you're hungry."

Boomer and Savage talked a little longer, decided what Boomer wanted, then Savage turned to Snake.

"Can I get you anything to eat?"

Snake shook his head, pushing thoughts of Jenny from his mind where they kept sneaking in, and focused on Savage. "I'm sorry. I was thinking. Bring me whatever you're bringing Boomer. I'll give him a tour then we'll be back."

Savage nodded. "You want the drinks now or with your food?"

"Now please," Snake said, conscious of how thirsty a long ride made him.

They waited while Savage went behind the bar and grabbed two bottles of water, then brought them back to them. Snake wished for a moment that he'd paid closer attention to what the new guy had ordered, water wasn't his favorite. But he'd make do until their meal was ready, then he'd ask for something else.

"Let's get started." Snake twisted the cap off his bottle and took a long drink. "This is the main room, we tend to gather here for social reasons, chatting, games, etc. There are women around sometimes, be careful about who you proposition though. Some of the members have old ladies that are welcome around the club, and you don't want to cross one of them. There are some that are available, take a day or two or ask. The old ladies won't get offended if you ask if they belong to anyone. The women who are available don't claim men who aren't theirs for fear of repercussions from the old ladies. That's the back room." He motioned to a set of double doors, one open, one closed. "We use it for all club meetings and anything sensitive. It's the only place we talk about that stuff." He headed for the metal stairs to one side of the room that led to the second floor and the private bedrooms. "Do you have a place in town yet?"

"I pick up the keys to my townhouse tomorrow, why?"

"We have rooms here. Several available. Some of the men keep a room here and a house, others one or the other. You're welcome to one if you need it. You have a place to stay tonight?"

"Not yet. I figured I'd find a motel nearby when I was ready to crash for the night."

"No need. I'll give you a room here. You can keep it long term for when you don't feel like the trip home or as a place to bring hookups, or not, it's up to you." He went to the linen closet where the bedding and the keys to the spare rooms were kept, handed Boomer a set of sheets, a blanket and pulled a key from the rack. That he kept to himself. "This way."

He led the new guy to the room indicated on the key and opened the door. "Room's clean, but you'll need to make your own bed. There should be towels in the bathroom." He motioned to the door on one wall that led to the attached bathroom. "You can keep it as long as you need, as long as you're with us that is. You leave the club or transfer to another chapter; you lose the room."

Boomer nodded and dropped the bedding Snake had given him a few minutes before onto the bed.

"Any questions?"

"A couple. What kind of meals are there? And when are they available?"

"Breakfast, lunch, dinner, nothing complicated, but there's always food in the place. If there's a prospect around you can get them to cook for you, or you can cook for yourself, just clean up any mess you make. The kitchen is well stocked. We also have regular gatherings, runs, family events, then there's club business stuff. It will be up to Sadist when you're pulled into that, at least as long as you're a prospect."

"As a prospect will I be put on bar duty? I assume that's what Savage is, a prospect."

"Possibly. It depends on your skills, what the club has going on and where we need you. Again, that's a call Sadist will make. Normally it would be Sadist and Tuck, but Tuck's out of hand for a few more months." He wasn't going to tell this guy exactly where Tuck was, that was club business, and this guy wasn't a member. Not yet. "Anything else?"

"Not that I can think of, not yet."

Snake nodded. "I'll leave you to settle in a bit. I'll be downstairs if you need anything. Don't forget Savage will have your lunch ready soon. Feel free to join me to eat if you'd like." With that, Snake turned and left. He finished the bottle of water on his way down the stairs and back to his table.

Questions about this new guy kept popping up in his mind, he might ask if he got a chance while they ate... at least it kept him from wondering about a girl he'd be better off keeping his distance from.

He didn't have long to wait. It only took a few minutes sitting alone at the table where he'd started before Savage came out of the kitchen carrying two plates. He set one in front of Snake and the other across the table from him.

"Anything else I can get you?" he asked.

"Another beer." Snake handed him the empty bottle that he'd left here when Boomer had come in.

"Coming right up." Savage took the bottle and left.

Snake looked down at what they would be eating and found a burger and fries. He was good with that. As long as it was hot and there was plenty, Snake wasn't too picky about what he ate. And it was a good thing, he couldn't cook worth shit so he ended up eating here or picking up something on his way home more often than not.

He picked up the burger and took a bite. It was better than he expected. He didn't know if it was something different that Savage did or if he just hadn't ordered a burger since he'd been back. But he'd have to do it again.

He was only a few bites in when Boomer sat and joined him. They ate in silence for a few minutes, then Snake let his curiosity get the better of him, though he was careful about the questions he asked, not wanting to be told to fuck off.

"How long was your trip out?" Snake asked as he picked up one of the fries that had come with his burger.

"It took me two days. I left yesterday but stopped in El Paso last night," Boomer said between bites.

So, he'd come from the east, but that didn't mean it was where he was originally from, just where he'd last been stationed.

"Can I ask where Boomer came from?"

The ghost of a smile curved the new guy's mouth.

"You can ask... that doesn't mean I'll answer." He took another bite then spoke again a minute later. "I joined the Army right out of high school. One thing and another I ended up a 12-bravo." He shrugged and picked up a fry. "Something about it just clicked. I could look at a situation, a problem and see where to place charges and how to shape them to bring them down with the least danger and most efficiency. Someone asked if I liked to see things go boom. It wasn't that, but I did like watching things happen the way I planned them." He met Snake's gaze. "It developed from there. Any time they needed something blown, someone would call get 'the boomer', and someone would look at me. In time it evolved to just Boomer." He shrugged again. "I got used to it."

"Combat engineer," Snake said with a slow nod. "I'm sure you have skills we can find a way to put to use. I take it Sadist knows that?"

"I'm sure he does. It was in the file I sent when I applied."

"You ever been to Tucson before?"

"Once, a long time ago. I was a kid, eight or nine, I think. I don't remember much other than some museum or something similar with a lot of stuffed animals." He scowled as if not sure if he was remembering things right.

"Ah. You mean like taxidermy animals, right?"

"Oh, yeah. Not like stuffies. They were dead animals that had been stuffed."

"That would be the Wildlife Museum. They've got more than just stuffed animals, but if you're not expecting it, it can be a bit much."

"A bit much." Boomer seemed to consider the phrase. "Yeah, I would say that. Especially as a kid." He seemed to shake himself. "Anyway. It's been a long time since I was in Tucson."

"No worries. Most of us have been around a while. I was here for a while, then gone for a couple years, but I've been back several months. If there's something you need and can't find or just don't want to look, ask one of the brothers. We'll probably be able to figure out where to get it."

"Sounds good."

They chatted a bit more, exchanging stories and bits about their lives, but not going into anything about the club. That was something Sadist or one of the officers would go over with him. Snake was just here to give him a basic tour and make sure he got a room.

After he'd finished eating, now that Boomer was settled in, he went back to work, walking next door to the mechanic shop where he worked for Mac when there was enough work, or they were a man short. Lately, he'd worked more often than not, and even though the shop was officially closed, he was in the middle of a job and wanted something to think about other than Jenny.

6

After work on Monday, Jenny sat in her car for a few minutes checking messages and letting the ache in her feet and back fade for a moment. It had been an insanely busy day, and she hadn't sat for more than a moment or two, since before lunch, and even that had been eaten on the fly. Now, she wanted nothing more than to get home, change into sweats and pass out.

Her stomach rumbled, reminding her she hadn't had time to eat more than a bite here or there on the run. Maybe she'd add eat a pint of ice cream to that list. No. There was none left in her freezer and the last thing she wanted to do was to stop and go into a store.

Still, she needed to eat. She mentally reviewed the places she could stop between the Dr.'s office where she worked and her place. What might take a different route and what options were out because there was no drive through. If she was going to get out of the car to get food, she'd be getting that ice cream, and she really didn't need it.

Whataburger. That would do. Now that she had decided that and a route home was determined, she started the car and hit the road.

She reached the burger place and placed her order then waited for her turn to pull up to the window, her mind drifting. Jenny couldn't help but wonder what Chuy and Jill were up to. Did she even want to know? Knowing her brother, probably not. But thoughts of him made her think about the wedding. She'd had a good time and not a little part of that was Snake.

She found herself smiling as she pulled up to the window, handed across her debit card and accepted her dinner and the card back.

Snake had been attentive, but not to the point that he was annoying or creepy. She wished, not for the first time since meeting him that someone like him would be interested in her as more than a partner for the ceremony or evening. She wished she could find a guy who cared as much as he seemed to and was interested in more than a hookup. Not that she minded the occasional hook up, but sometimes you wanted someone who cared. Or at least cared about more than their next blow job.

A horn blasting nearby called her attention back to the fact that she was driving. She looked around, frantic for just a moment, until she realized they were honking at someone two lanes over.

A deep breath helped calm her heart rate and she pushed everything out of her mind but the traffic and making it home safely.

⚜ ⚜

J enny cleaned up her mess after eating and wandered into the living room, where she sat on the couch, turned on the TV and let her mind wander.

She didn't know how much time had passed when she found herself lying on the sofa, feet propped up on one arm as she stared up at the ceiling and wondered if this was what her life would be like from now on. Going to work, coming home with her feet and back aching, then watching TV alone until it was time to go to bed and start all over again the next

day. There had to be more to it than this. There had to be more
to life than working to live and existing in between shifts. But
when would she get there?

Jenny took a deep breath and let it out in a rush. This kind
of thinking would get her nowhere. She needed to take control
of her life and not just let life happen to her. She needed a plan.
She didn't know what yet, but she needed to come up with a
plan for what she wanted and how to get it.

It wasn't that she had been floundering. No, she'd gone to
school to become a medical assistant, they made decent money,
and she'd taken the extra courses to become a phlebotomist
as well, just as a precaution. The way she saw it, the more
marketable skills she had, the more employable she was, and
the more possibilities were available. She'd been working for a
couple years and felt like she was doing okay. She'd just moved
into her own place, it was tiny, but it was hers. And she liked
her job. Neither of those was a small thing but somehow she
felt like something was missing. She didn't have to think about
what it was. Chuy's wedding had driven the point home with
startling clarity.

She was alone.

While she'd spent years telling others she didn't need a man
in her life, and in general it was true. She didn't need anyone...
but it made for a lonely life, and she wanted someone to share
her life, her time, the enjoyable experiences and to lean on
when it came to the hard times. And nights where she was too
tired to do anything but sit and be a vegetable until bedtime
drove that loneliness home.

This line of thinking was getting her nowhere. She huffed
a sigh, got up and went into the bedroom. When she'd been
looking for an apartment, she'd only had a couple of require-
ments, an actual bedroom. She didn't want a studio so that she
had one living space, and a bathtub. She could shower every
day to get clean if she had to, but when she was particularly
down or cold, she wanted to be able to sink into a tub of hot

water and soak. She didn't know why that one thing was a big deal to her, even if she didn't do it for months, then she'd have a string of baths as she tried to get something out of her system or figure out a solution.

That was where she was headed now. She turned on the tap and adjusted the temperature before dumping in a couple handfuls of Epsom salts. It would help her sore muscles and she liked the way it made her skin feel. While the tub filled, Jenny made sure she had a towel, and went into the bedroom and grabbed the book she'd left on her nightstand the night before.

A quick glance at her watch before she took it off told her she had a couple hours before she had to go to bed, not that she planned to be in the tub that long, but it was good to know she had time if she lost track of time while reading. She finished stripping then stepped into the tub, hissing at the slight sting of the hot water. She adjusted the water running into the tub again, then sank down into the nearly steaming water and closed her eyes a moment. The heat seeped into her muscles and then into her bones, taking away the slight ache that the chill in the air had caused.

After a few minutes, she shut off the water, leaned over and picked up her book and quickly lost herself in the story. At least lost in the book she wasn't fretting about her own life and wondering why she wasn't doing better or at least differently.

7

A t the end of the day, Snake washed up at the sink in the shop, but it wasn't enough. He'd wrestled with a stuck oil plug for twenty minutes this afternoon and when it had finally come loose had sprayed him with some of the blackest oil he'd ever seen.

He'd gotten as much of it off as he could at the time, but he still felt dirt and grit on his face and in his hair. He considered going home, but didn't want to wait any longer for a shower. Instead, he walked across the parking lot to the club house. Inside, Savage was behind the counter.

"We have the stuff for a plate of enchiladas?" he asked standing next to the bar.

"We do."

"Good. I'm gonna head up to my room and shower, can I get a plate of red enchiladas when I come back down? And a beer now would be nice."

"What kind?"

"Anything in a bottle."

The prospect reached into a cooler and pulled out a Coors stubby bottle, popped the top, and handed it across the bar.

"Thanks."

"Fifteen minutes or what?"

Snake ran a hand through his hair as he took a pull from the beer. His hand came away gritty and oil stained. He pulled a face.

"Better give me thirty. It might take a while to get this shit off."

"You got it." Savage turned back to where he was wiping down the counter and cleaning dishes.

Snake took his beer, climbed the stairs, and let himself into the room he kept here. Snake had spent a few weeks living here when he'd first come back from Texas. Now he just kept it in case he decided to spend the night some time. He made a mental note to replace those as he set the beer on the small table next to the bed and stripped out of the oil spattered ones, tossing them in a corner to deal with later. He then picked up the beer and took it into the bathroom with him. It had been a hell of a day, and he was going to enjoy the cold beer while he tried to get rid of some of the oil and grit.

B y the time he made it back downstairs, his dinner was ready and sitting on the bar in front of the stool he preferred. He lifted the empty beer bottle to get Savage's attention and let him know he wanted another, then sat at the bar and inhaled the tantalizing, spicy aroma coming from the plate.

"Mind if I join you?" a voice came from behind him and a little to the right as Snake took the first bite of his dinner. He twisted around, hurried to swallow, and motioned to the seat beside him. It was Sadist.

"Sure," Snake said once he could do so without dumping his meal all over the place. "I wasn't expecting to see you tonight." He turned back to the counter, picked up his fresh drink and took a sip. "I figured you'd be home with Beth."

"I'm headed that way, but I wanted to stop by and check in on the new guy. What did you think?"

Snake shrugged. "I only spent about fifteen minutes with him. I don't know what to think. Not yet."

"I'm not looking for a comprehensive evaluation of his character," Sadist said as he rolled his eyes. "I just want your impression of him."

Snake let his head tilt to one side as he considered the question. "He seems decent enough. From his MOS, I'd say he's responsible enough, and likely steady. Do you have any ideas what kind of job you're going to give him?"

Sadist glanced at Snake then over to Savage and back again. "Do you not think bartending for the club is a good option?" He watched him with a single lifted brow.

"I'm not trying to tell you how to run the club, but I'm sure he could handle the job. I just think it's not the best use of him and his skillset."

Sadist scowled. "Skillset?"

Snake frowned. "Do you not know?" But how was that possible? Sadist had the file, and surely, he'd read it before allowing the man to come. "He's a combat engineer. I'm sure there are things he could do for the club, things he could help with, that no one else has the skill to handle."

Sadist lifted his brow so they both came close to his hairline but didn't say anything more as he considered the revelation.

"You may be right." He turned away, a crease forming between his brows as he turned to scan the room. "Any idea where he is?"

Snake turned and scanned the room himself. "Not here. Maybe up in his room." He gave the Vice President the number of the room Snake had given Boomer, then continued. "I'm not sure though. I gave him a room, we ate, then I went over to the shop and got some work in. I got back about forty-five minutes ago but I've spent most of that scrubbing off the grease. He didn't say anything about going anywhere tonight, but I didn't ask either."

Sadist nodded slowly, his gaze still playing over the room, as if he was only half listening to Snake. "Let me know if anything comes up or you think of anything else you think I should know."

"Will do."

"And don't forget. There's a meeting tonight at nine. I expect you to be there."

Sadist slid off the bar stool and went to talk to another brother, Snake turned his attention back to his dinner. He'd forgotten about the meeting. He motioned to Savage for another drink. With having to stay, or come back, for the meeting that made his decision as to where to sleep tonight. He wasn't going to bother going back to the house tonight.

He took a deep breath and let it out in a rush before pulling out his phone and setting a reminder to take his grubby clothes home and bring more clean ones next trip. He needed to keep more than one outfit here. Maybe two or three days' worth would be a good idea. He shook his head and pushed the thought of his mind. He'd decide later.

※※※※※ ※※※※※

S nake was sitting at the table in the back room when Sadist came in, looked around and went to the head of the table. He sat and watched as a few more brothers trickled in then motioned to Dumbass to close the door.

The men chatted and talked in low voices until the door was locked and Sadist cleared this throat.

"I know Gizmo's not here, but we've got some business we need to take care of, and Ruger has his proxy so let's get down to business."

All the brothers in the room, which was nearly all the fully patched members of the Tucson Chapter, went quiet. Several leaned forward in their chairs, some leaning on the long, heavy oak table that stood for their meeting table, while others leaned back so they could see around their neighbors.

"First. You're all aware of the official formation of the Gillette Chapter, correct?" Sadist waited a moment then when no one spoke up, continued. "I'm not going to rehash old business but because of the formation of the Gillette Chapter, and those who are up there, either temporarily or permanently, we find ourselves critically low on patched brothers. By critically low I mean we don't have enough men to continue some of our typical operations." He paused and looked around the room, as if waiting for someone to speak up or ask questions.

No one did. They all remained silent and listening.

"With our current numbers we don't have the personnel to continue our people moving operations. We're going to have to shift to less sensitive cargo. Though that comes with risks too." He scanned the room as if looking for dessert, but there was nothing. "I've got some leads. We're going to be moving weapons maybe a few other things, but not drugs. I think we all know where Tuck and I stand on moving that shit." His eyes scanned the room again.

Snake knew, and assumed most of his brothers did too. He glanced around and found several of his brothers nodding agreement. Not only would they not participate in moving that shit, they also actively worked to get rid of anyone bringing it in or through the city. With Tucson's proximity to the border, it was a constant and never-ending battle.

"Shifting cargo is only part of our strategy to keep things going while things are tight. We're also bringing in more prospects than normal, and we'll be voting more often on how often to patch them in." He waited while there was some chatter, but it quickly died down and he continued. "We're going to start with that today. Today we're going to vote on Savage and Sackett. You all know how it's done. We'll do them separately and you can say yea or no, but you can't abstain. We need at least 80% yea to patch someone in. Everyone understand?" Sadist's eyes scanned the room making sure there was no misunderstanding.

"We're going to start with Sackett. Is there anyone here who wants to say something in his favor?"

Ruger cleared his throat. "I will say he's done everything we've asked of him, and with no complaint. He pitches in and does whatever he's asked and often doesn't wait to be asked but does whatever he sees that needs to get done. I think he's been a valuable member of the club, even as a prospect and don't see why he wouldn't be even more valuable as a brother." Ruger turned to Sadist and nodded, indicating he was done.

"Anyone else?" Sadist asked. He gave it a moment, then when no one spoke up, he spoke again. "All right, does anyone want to say anything against him?"

No one spoke and few even moved.

"All right. We'll vote then. Everyone who votes yea, to patch in Sackett, raise your hand."

Hands went up around the room, Ruger stood and with two fingers held together, counted the hands.

"You can lower them now." Sadist turned to Ruger and lifted one brow in silent question.

Ruger shook his head, and Sadist turned back to the rest of the brothers.

"We've got over 80%, there is no reason to ask for the nays. Next, we'll move on to Savage. He's not been with us quite as long, but I want to take a vote on him anyway. First does anyone have anything to say in his favor?"

A couple of men spoke up, they listed general things but even Snake had to admit he didn't know the man well. He'd been back a few months, and he didn't know why but the only things he knew about the prospect was that he was damn good in the kitchen and not bad behind the bar.

When Sadist asked for people to say anything they had against him being patched in, Stretch spoke up and said most of what Snake had been thinking, so he didn't bother to say it himself.

"Anyone else have anything to say?" Sadist asked a few minutes later. When no one spoke up, he went through the vote process again. This time they went all the way through with the nays as well as the yeas. "All right. We're almost even on votes and it seems that's because we don't know him well enough to trust him, at least not yet. You all know how this works. Just because he wasn't voted in doesn't mean we cut him loose. It will mean that we don't vote on him again until the next opening. Because of circumstances, I'll say that will be in three months. Hopefully he'll have more going for him then."

There was a little more talk, discussion of things that couldn't happen outside this room.

"I have one more thing," Sadist said at the head of the table. "We still have several months until Tuck's return, but that isn't my concern. We've got a new prospect, Boomer. I'm not sure how many of you have met him yet, but I'm not putting him to work manning the bar here. I'm not saying he wouldn't be able to handle it, but he was a combat engineer and I think tending bar might not be the best use of his skills. I haven't yet decided what I'll put him to doing, but I'm willing to take suggestions." His gaze went from man to man in the room and he kept a solemn face as he continued. "And I mean sincere suggestions, not things to screw with me or him." It was clear to Snake their VP knew the kind of sense of humor too many of the brothers had.

Snake rolled his lips inward and bit them, but he couldn't keep the amusement from showing in his eyes. Ruger caught the look and met his gaze, one brow lifting in question. Snake shook his head, indicating he wasn't sharing, at least not now. He might talk to Ruger privately later. Maybe he'd tell Sadist, but Snake wouldn't be making the suggestion.

Sadist called the business of the meeting over and closed the meeting, but they didn't open the door right away. Instead, informal chatter filled the room.

"When will Gizmo be back? I have a couple of things I need researched," Stretch said from his seat, looking around in case anyone knew the answer.

"Come by here tomorrow," Ruger leaned back in his chair until Snake worried it would tip over backward. "Krissi is taking over tech officer duties while Giz is gone. She can do nearly everything he does, though she's not as adroit at designing security systems."

Stretch didn't say anything, but his expression made it clear he didn't like going to their treasurer's woman for his tech needs. Snake wasn't sure if it was because she was a woman, because she wasn't a brother, or because of who her father was. Snake wasn't about to ask either Stretch or Ruger. He'd heard about what had happened while he was gone, but wasn't willing to bring it up. He just listened to all the gossip as it went on around him. There was some discussion as to when to tell Sackett he'd been voted in and when they would have a patch party for him.

It took probably twenty minutes after the meeting wrapped up before someone unlocked the door and left. Snake made his way out to the main room and signaled to Savage for a fresh drink, then found a seat at one of the empty tables. He'd sit out here a while, listen to the chatter, maybe watch something on one of the TVs in the corner, then call it a night and go upstairs.

8

J enny threw her legs over the edge of the bed and groaned. She didn't want to get up. She'd been having a delightful dream that she still resented getting interrupted, not that she could remember what she'd been dreaming, only that she didn't want to leave it.

With a deep breath, she forced herself to her feet and shuffled into the bathroom. After she'd completed her necessities, she staggered into the kitchen and fumbled through putting a coffee pod in the pot and staring at the machine.

Two minutes later, she was more awake and cursing herself for forgetting to put a cup under the coffee maker. Now she was cleaning up the mess, and had that much longer to wait for the caffeine that kick started her brain into functionality.

Could she live without it? Yes, but she would be slower, cranky and it would make the day harder for her and the people she worked with. No one wanted that. Better for her to clean up the mess, make a fresh cup and get on with her day.

Finally, cup in hand and already half gone, she started another cup and went to take a shower. It wasn't the best start of the day, but she wasn't about to let it ruin her day. Maybe by the time she'd showered and had her second cup of coffee she'd be better equipped to handle whatever came up today.

S he'd almost made it to work when it happened. She was driving along, paying as much attention to the traffic as usual, nothing seemed out of place until someone ignored the red light as she was crossing the intersection, they t-boned her car, sending her careening into the flow of traffic on the opposite side of the road and smashing her around like one of those old toy cars Chuy used to have that had parts that flipped and made them look like they'd been in a demolition derby.

When the world stopped moving, Jenny sat for a moment, blinking, and trying to figure out what had happened.

"Are you all right? Ma'am, are you okay?"

The tone of the voice made her think maybe this wasn't the first time she'd been asked. She looked up and realized there were flashing lights and she realized she must have been out of it for more than a few seconds. There was no way the police had arrived any quicker than five minutes, possibly longer.

"I think so." She blinked again, and tried to do a mental inventory and figure out if she was hurt. "How long?"

"How long what?" the unfamiliar voice asked.

"How long since the accident?"

"Just a few minutes. I was a couple blocks away when I got the call. It hasn't been long. Can you give me your name?" The voice was kind, and professional but no-nonsense.

"Jenny, I mean Juanita Martinez."

"Is there anyone we can call for you?"

She started to say her brother, but stopped before she got it out.

Chuy was on his honeymoon, and she didn't want to mess that up for him. No. He gave her a number for emergencies while he was gone, but she didn't remember it off hand. She would have to pull up his messages and find it. Jenny shook her head and the world seemed to spin. *Don't do that again,* she told herself as she grimaced and stilled.

"No, I'll get my phone and find who needs to be called. Do you see my bag?" She didn't turn but reached toward her passenger's seat where she'd left it. She didn't find the bag but encountered crumpled metal instead. That wasn't right. She wanted to say something about the state of her car, but words didn't come to her mind off hand.

"I don't, but let me see if I can find it from the other side."

She heard a movement, then a breeze reached her face. Jenny blinked several times and looked around without moving her head or neck. That hadn't been fun the one time she'd done it.

"I found it!" The voice came from the other side of the car.

There was a sound of cloth against metal, and she hoped whoever was there was trying to reach her bag so they could give it to her and that it wasn't some jerk who just wanted to steal. Nothing seemed too badly hurt, but she ached all over. She wasn't sure if she'd lost consciousness, but knew since she'd lost time, the EMTs would want to take her in. The way she felt right now, she didn't think she would be arguing. Still, she needed to find her phone and call someone. Not Chuy, but someone. Maybe that guy from the wedding. What had his name been? Something strange like the name Chuy used with them, and had brought to mind something scaley, Fish? No, she hadn't thought slime, and fish made her think slimy. Slither. Snake. That was it.

"Here's your bag. Can you take it, or do you want me to find something in it for you?"

"Let me see it?" she said, careful not to turn her head.

Her bag came into view through the shattered window to her left and seemed to lower into her lap. Jenny didn't even have to look down to start digging. Once she'd felt the bag and figured out which way it sat in her lap, she had the phone in her hand in seconds. As that was all it took her to find the pocket where she kept the device. She didn't bother moving her bag but lifted her phone into her line of sight and started navigating to her brother's messages.

"Is everyone else okay?" she asked while trying to find the number Chuy had sent her.

"I'm not convinced you're okay," the voice said.

"I'm not either, but I'll do for now. Go check on the others. I'm not going anywhere and while I ache, I don't think I'm seriously hurt."

"Are you sure?"

"I am. I'm going to find this number and make a call, that's all."

"If you're sure. but don't sleep either. I don't know how long you were out, but I don't like that. I want to make sure you get seen."

"I'm not going to argue with that, but go make sure everyone else is okay." She thumbed through the messages and found the number. Waiting until the man who'd been at her window left, she hit the number and told her phone to dial it, then put the phone on speaker so she didn't have to try to hold it to her head and waited for someone to answer.

It didn't take long. Someone picked up on the second ring.

"This is Sadist." The voice on the other end of the line was clear and brisk, businesslike.

She blinked, she hadn't expected that name and wasn't sure how to react to it.

"Hello?"

"Hi. You're a friend of my brother's I think."

"Who is your brother?"

"Chuy, but I think you call him Gizmo."

"That would make you Jenny?" His voice turned more gentle.

"It would. I'm sorry. I need help, but I don't want to interrupt Chuy's honeymoon." She heard her voice shake and fought to keep it steady.

"What do you need help with, Jenny?"

"I—I've been in an accident and I'm pretty sure they'll be taking me to the hospital soon. I don't know what to do."

"About what?"

"About everything. My car will need to get towed, I'm sure it's totaled." She hadn't seen it yet but the fact that she could reach out and touch metal told her a lot. "And I don't know how I'll get home."

"Where are you?" His voice had turned even more gentle.

Jenny blinked and tried to remember where she'd been when everything had changed, and the world had started spinning.

"Ina." She wasn't sure about the cross street, not yet.

"That's a good start. I'll send someone up that way." There was some commotion on the other end of the line.

She struggled to remember where she'd been on Ina. Still not sure, she looked around, turning her head slowly so she didn't set the world to spinning again.

There, a street sign. Now she just needed to be able to read it. It took a second before her vision cleared enough to be able to read the sign.

"You still there, Jenny?" The voice sounded concerned, and she thought it might not be the first time he'd asked her.

"I am. I was trying to figure out the cross street. I'm at Ina and Mona Lisa."

"Good to know. Up there they'll take you to Northwest. I'll send a truck up to get your car and someone to the hospital to be with you there. Are you hurt?"

"I don't know. I don't think so, but I'm still sitting in my car. Someone handed me my purse so I could find my phone but I'm a little shaken up and out of it."

"But not too out of it that you remembered not to call Gizmo. That's good."

"I know. Anyone you send to the hospital won't be allowed back to see me until I'm released."

"Don't worry about that. I'll take care of it."

Her head was starting to ache, and she didn't want to think too much so she let it go. "The ambulance just got here. I probably need to go soon. I just didn't know who else to call, especially with Chuy gone."

"No worries, Jenny. You did the right thing. we'll have someone with you soon, then you can rest and get better. Even if you're not hurt, you'll be sore for a few days."

"Ma'am? Ma'am. Can I talk to you a moment?" A deep male voice came from her left, outside the car.

"Someone is here. I've got to go."

"No problem. We'll see you soon."

She disconnected the call and let the phone fall back into the purse still sitting open in her lap. She turned slowly until a man in some kind of uniform, she thought it was an EMT came into the edge of her view.

"Yes?"

"I'm Jacob, I'm here to help you get out of there and make sure you're okay. If we need to, I'll take you to the hospital. Can you tell me how you're feeling?"

Jenny closed her eyes a moment and took a deep breath. "Nothing actively hurts. At least not more than anything else. I do ache all over a bit, and turning my head too fast makes me dizzy."

"That's good to know. Have you tried to get out at all? How does your neck feel?"

"Neck is a little sore, but not unbearable. I haven't tried to get out. I didn't even retrieve my bag myself, someone reached in the other side and brought it to me."

"It's good that you're moving your hands with no difficulty. How about your feet? Can you see them?"

She slowly moved her head so she could look down into the floorboard. "I can see them."

"Can you move them?"

She tried to flex her ankles, and her feet both moved, but she couldn't help crying out as a sharp pain shot up her right leg.

"What is it?" Jacob asked.

She closed her eyes and took another deep breath as she let the pain wash through her and pass.

"My leg. I can move my feet, but there's something wrong with my right leg. It hurts a lot when I move my foot."

"All right. That's good to know. Can you look at me again?" His voice was calm and patient. She thought he was trying to keep her from panicking.

She turned, careful not to move too quickly, until a face hovering somewhere near where her mirror was supposed to be was the center of her vision. It took her a moment to realize he must be squatting next to the car to be closer to eye level with her. Unbidden, the wish that Snake was there and helping her popped into her head. She pushed it away and tried to focus on Jacob. He was the one here to help her and wishing for others would do no good.

"Yes?"

"The first step is to get you out of the car. We're going to do a few things to make sure you don't have a spinal injury or if you do, that we don't make it worse. Bear with me a few minutes as we get things ready, okay?"

"All right."

"Have you tried opening the door yet?"

"No. I hadn't gotten that far when the guy who gave me my purse showed up and told me to stay put. I think he's a police officer, but I can't be sure."

"That's okay. Let me try it now, then I'll get my partner over here and we'll see what we can do to get you out of here. Can you put the car in park and unlock the door for me?"

Jenny did as he asked, doing her best to move as little as possible because she learned just shifting the car into park, that even that little bit of movement sent bolts of pain through her leg.

"Done," she said after doing both things.

He tried to open her door. It took several tugs and a couple minutes, but he did get it open. Now the real work began.

9

"Yo?" Snake said in answering his phone.

"You busy?" Sadist's voice came over the line.

"Not particularly. I finished the last job Mac had for me about twenty minutes ago and was trying to decide how to spend my afternoon."

"I need you take the tow truck and pick up a car."

Something in the other man's voice set off warning bells in Snake's mind. "Is everything okay?"

"I'm not sure yet. Gizmo's sister has been in an accident. She just called me. She was with it enough to remember not to call him, but I think she might be more hurt than she was letting on. I need you to go get her car, she said the ambulance had just gotten there as we were hanging up. I'm going to send Beth or one of the women to the hospital and call Kinard to see if he's on shift."

Snake's chest ached and for a moment he thought his heart might have stopped beating. Then he heard the familiar tha-whump in his ears, as if the world had faded and all heard was his heartbeat.

"I'll take care of the car, just tell me where." He got to the intersection and all the information the VP had and headed out to the tow truck, thankful he hadn't headed into the club-house and ordered a drink yet.

What he didn't tell the other man was that he would be picking up the car, bringing it back to the lot then he'd head over to the hospital himself. He didn't yet know if he'd take the time to unload the car. What he did know was that he wouldn't breathe easy until he saw Jenny for himself and could be sure she was okay with his own eyes. He hated the thought of her hurt and alone, and she'd told him the other night she'd never met any of the Souls. Snake was willing to bet that meant she also didn't know any of the old ladies and while she might be glad for a little female company, what good would that do if they were all strangers to her?

Not that he was much better, but at least he'd spent an evening with her, talking and getting to know her and he'd liked her. That had to be better than strangers, right? He told himself it was just concern for his brother's sister. He'd do the same for any of his brothers. But deep inside, he knew he was lying to himself. He'd worry about that after he was sure Jenny would be okay.

He pulled up to the intersection and shook his head. Aside from the emergency vehicles, which kept most of the intersection closed and redirected the much-narrowed flow of traffic through the area, there were two vehicles in the accident. One was a pickup that was at least thirty years old. The front end was damaged, and it appeared to Snake that this was probably the at fault vehicle. He didn't know what Jenny's car was, but he hoped she'd been in that one because the damage to the small SUV type vehicle was enough to make his teeth ache in sympathy for whoever had been in it. The entire passenger's side was smashed in, leaving him little doubt that anyone sitting on that side of the vehicle wouldn't have survived.

He eased the large flatbed truck out of the way and climbed down so he could talk to the officers. To one side he spotted an ambulance with someone on a gurney outside the vehicle, he couldn't see much about the person, but they had long dark hair that reminded him of Jenny, so he headed that way first.

It was Jenny on the gurney. His heart seemed to stutter, and his stomach tightened then turned over. He stayed silent, just stepped closer and picked up the hand closest to him. She looked over to see who it was, but kept talking to the police officer on the other side of the gurney. She smiled when she spotted him, then took his hand and squeezed it as she turned back to the officer and continued explaining.

After a moment, the officer turned to him.

"And you are?"

"I'm here with the tow truck." He jerked one thumb over his shoulder at the truck. "But I know her and wanted to be sure she is okay before I pick up her car."

"I'm okay. Or at least I will be." Jenny squeezed his hand again but didn't release him.

The officer nodded then spoke. "We're not quite ready to move the vehicles yet. Give us a bit to finish with pictures, measurements and such then we'll let you load up."

"No problem. I'm going to talk to her a moment before they load her up, then I'll come look for you."

The officer nodded, folded his notebook closed, then opened it again as if it was a habit, he didn't realize he was doing, then turned and headed for another officer. Snake turned back to Jenny.

"How bad are you hurt?" He didn't bother trying to keep the concern from his face.

"I'll be okay, I'm sure. My leg hurts." She motioned to her legs that were covered with a thin blanket, then looked back at him and blinked. "But that's about it."

"We can't be sure until we get some kind of imaging on that leg and your head." One of the EMT's came up on the other side of the gurney and began running straps across the top over her legs and abdomen, so Jenny wouldn't be thrown around the vehicle if they had to make sharp turns or got into an accident of their own.

"What's this about your head?"

Jenny waved her other hand and shook her head. "It's nothing. The accident stunned me, and I was out of it for a few minutes."

The EMT frowned at her but didn't say anything.

"Out of it or out? There is a difference you know," Snake asked with a frown. He couldn't believe the paramedic wasn't asking these questions.

She didn't answer. Snake watched her for a moment, but couldn't decide if she was being stubborn or didn't know.

"Where are you taking her?" This time he addressed his question to the EMT.

"Northwest. It's closest and not on bypass."

"Good. I'll let the rest of the family know."

"You family?" the paramedic asked.

"Sure am, but I'm really here to get her car." Snake turned his attention back to Jenny. "I'll take care of your car, it will be at the shop when you're ready for it, but from the looks of it, that may not be for a while yet." He let his gaze skim her face, then down the rest of her body. When he looked back at her face, he found her watching him with a confused look on her face, but at least she didn't ask what shop or what the hell he was talking about. He had her tell him which car was hers, and unfortunately it wasn't the pickup he'd hoped she'd been driving.

Snake noticed the officer who seemed to be in charge look at his truck then around the scene as if looking for someone. From his body language, Snake thought it might be him. He covered one of Jenny's hands with one of his and squeezed briefly.

"I'll find you soon. Either at the hospital or at home, but I've got to get busy." He released her hand and headed for the officer to see if they were ready for him to move the car. "You looking for me?" he said as he approached the officer.

"I think so. You driving that?" Officer Jenkins, according to his name tag, motioned to Snake's truck.

"I am."

"Good. We're ready to move that one." Jenkins motioned to the truck with a smashed front end with a rainbow of fluids dripping from under the twisted metal that had been the engine compartment.

"Sorry. I'm here for that one." Snake indicated the other vehicle. Jenny's car had been hit on the passenger's side, and he knew enough about cars to know the frame was likely bent and it would most likely be totaled, no matter what he'd told her.

Jenkin's frowned. "You weren't sent out by dispatch?"

"No, I came because she's family, or close enough."

Jenkins' frown turned to a confused scowl. "You don't want to go with her?"

Snake shook his head. "I talked to her. I know she's mostly okay. I'll call someone to meet her at the hospital, at least until I can get there."

Jenkins' scowl disappeared and he nodded. "We're almost ready to move hers, then you can head out."

Snake nodded, then glanced over at Jenny to see how she was doing and found the EMT's loading her into the back of the bus. Instead of going over and holding them up, Snake moved to stand out of the way and pulled out his phone.

The first thing he did was to shoot off a message to Sadist letting him know the ambulance was about to leave and where it was headed. After the message was sent, he glanced around again and wondered how much longer he would be here and if he could make it to the hospital before they released Jenny?

He couldn't decide which he hoped for. On one hand, he wanted to see her, but on the other, the last thing he wanted was for her to be more seriously hurt than he'd originally thought.

He had no claim on her. No right to ask someone else to do this so he could be with her, still, that was exactly what he wanted to do.

No.

He would do what he'd been asked to do. He would take care of her car, then find out where she was and see her then. That decision didn't stop him from shooting a second text out, this one to Kinard to see of his brother was working today... if he was, he would be in the very emergency room where she was headed.

10

Everything seemed so surreal to Jenny as she sat semi-reclining and strapped to the gurney on her way to the hospital. She answered the EMT's questions on autopilot as she wondered about her feelings when she'd spotted Snake. That spurt of relief and excitement confused her.

Had it been because he was the only person there that she'd even met before? Or was it because it was *him*? She wasn't sure and didn't know how to figure it out.

It seemed very little time had passed when they pulled into the ambulance bay and opened the rear doors. The jarring and jostling as they unloaded her hurt more than when they'd loaded her. Or maybe the adrenaline was wearing off. She clenched her teeth to keep from making any noise, though she didn't know why she was so determined to remain silent. She knew the EMTs weren't being rough on purpose or trying to hurt her, maybe that was what kept her quiet.

The EMTs were met by a couple of people in scrubs, they exchanged a lot of information that mostly seemed like gibberish to her. Though with her job it should make more sense than it did. Was that a sign she'd hit her head harder than she'd thought? Then they moved her from the gurney to a bed in one of what seemed like a dozen or more rooms and the EMTs faded away. Or maybe she just lost track of them.

Time seemed to blur, the faces of the people talking to her, asking questions, poking, and prodding at what seemed like every bruise she'd had in her life had gone fuzzy.

She didn't know how much time had passed before she saw a face she recognized. But she couldn't remember where she'd seen him or if she'd ever heard his name.

"Good afternoon, Jenny. How are you feeling?" the man who seemed familiar asked.

"Not my best. It seems like the longer I'm here, the more I hurt."

"That's sometimes how it goes. Tell me more about your pain. I'm sure you've been asked several times already, but on a scale of one to ten, ten being the worst pain you can imagine, can you rate your pain for me?" He was friendly, but still professional. She wished she could remember if she'd heard his name, but it was a blank, and she couldn't focus on the badge dangling from the lapel of his white coat enough to read his name.

"Um. I'd say six to seven. It hurts pretty bad, but I'm sure it could be worse."

"Okay tell me more about what happened and where it hurts." He met her gaze, and she couldn't help but wonder again where she'd seen him and what his name was.

"Jenny?"

The sound of her name made her shake her head and blink, realizing he'd been talking to her, and she hadn't been paying attention.

"Sorry. What was that?"

"The paramedics said the accident possibly knocked you out. Do you remember that?"

She shook her head. "No. I don't. I remember being dazed. In fact, I think I'm still not thinking quite right."

"Let me take a look at your eyes and check a couple other things." He moved closer and looked at one eye, then the other with a bright light that made it feel like the light was a spike being driven into her head. She fought not to squeeze her eyes closed and turn away, as he said he needed to see.

He turned and said something to someone else in the room, someone she didn't see and before she could register what he'd said he lifted the rails on his side of the bed while someone lifted the one on the other and the bed started moving.

Lights flashed and she lost track of what was happening. The last thing she remembered was being moved from one table to another and the pain in her head and leg, then everything went black.

❧❧❧❧❧❧ ❧❧❧❧❧❧

The first thing Jenny became aware of was a soft, rhythmic beep. She didn't know where it was coming from, but it was close. And after a few minutes she knew if she didn't get it shut off, she was going to find something to throw at it. Her whole body hurt but the beeping seemed to bore into her skull until it was all she could think about.

It took her a moment to pry her eyes open. When she managed to get them to open a crack, she was thankful the room was dim, and the light didn't seem to stab her in the brain like the beeping. She took several more breaths as she tried to look around, but she couldn't see much.

Dotted ceiling tiles, inset florescent lighting, a door with a long thin window, and another door with no window on the other side. Slowly things began to come back to her.

The accident. The ambulance. Snake. The man she still couldn't place. She had to be in the hospital, but how long had she been here? Had someone called Chuy and ruined his honeymoon? She hoped not.

The beeping continued. She had to find it and get it turned off. Maybe a nurse would help? She turned her head, trying to find the source and found the simple movement took more effort than she could ever remember.

"Jenny?" a voice asked, softly, barely more than a whisper. "Are you awake?"

"Ye—" She had to stop. Her voice had come out as no more than a dry rasp. She tried to clear her throat, but her mouth was so dry. "Water?" she whispered, hoping whoever was there would help her.

11

Snake didn't know how long he'd been sitting in her hospital room, and he didn't care. Sadist had told him someone would come relieve him, but Snake had told him not to bother. He wouldn't be going home until she was awake. He wasn't sure he would be going home even then.

Fuck. How had he missed that she was more hurt than she'd seemed? And now, several hours after she'd gotten out of surgery, she still hadn't woken up. The nurse who came in at least once an hour to check on her had said it was normal, and not to worry, not yet, but that didn't help.

He had seen her on the scene, he should have realized something wasn't right. Especially after what she'd said about being out.

The sound of fabric sliding against fabric drew his attention.

"Jenny?" Snake kept his voice soft in case he'd been wrong, and the sound hadn't come from the bed. He leaned forward, and found her eyes open, searching.

"Ye—" Her voice was barely more than a whisper and the word barely started before she stopped and made a face. "Water?" she whispered.

Snake stood, picked up the plastic cup with a straw the nurse had left for her and held it close so she could take a sip.

"Thank you," she said after a couple brief sips. "The hospital?" she asked, a confused frown creasing her brow. "How bad?" she asked after he nodded, confirming her conclusion.

"Pretty bad. You have a head injury that I wasn't aware of at the scene. The good news is that Kinard caught it shortly after you arrived in the ER. He got you in for testing and then into surgery. You were pretty beat up by the accident, but he says you'll be okay, it will just take time to heal."

Jenny closed her eyes and seemed to relax for a moment. "Kinard? Was he at Chuy's wedding?"

Snake felt the ghost of a smile curve his mouth as she found something other than herself to focus on.

"Yeah, he was at the wedding. He's one of our brothers. I know there are a lot of us to keep the names straight when you've just met us all." Despite what he told her, he couldn't help but be impressed that she'd recognized his brother, especially with a head wound, even if she hadn't been sure where she'd seen him before.

"What else?" she asked.

"Broken leg, they had to do surgery to set it, but Kinard said it was a clean break and should heal without complications. That is if you follow instructions better than we do." He couldn't help giving her a wry grin, even though her eyes were closed, and she wouldn't see it.

"Did they say when I can get out of here?"

"Sorry, baby, no. The docs have been in and out but wouldn't give any prognosis until you woke up. Speaking of, let me let the nurse know you're awake." He stood and went to the door. He stood there a moment until he caught the attention of one of the nurses, waved to get her to come in, then went back to the chair he'd spent the last several hours in.

He wasn't about to leave her, not yet. Not until he was sure she would be okay.

Snake didn't know why he felt so protective of her. It wasn't just because she was his brother's sister, that was for sure. Still, he chose not to look too closely at it, not yet. Maybe not ever.

"She'll be in soon, I'm sure. How bad's it hurt?"

Her face scrunched in a manner he was learning meant she was thinking.

"It hurts. Everywhere."

Without thinking about it he reached over and covered one of her hands, trying to make her feel not so alone. To his surprise, she turned the hand over and curled her fingers around his. After a moment, she wove her fingers into his. He wasn't sure he should be doing this, but she seemed to relax some. Maybe the touch of someone, even a stranger like him, made her feel not so alone. Not knowing if that was what it was or something else, he wasn't about to pull away and take what little comfort she might have while lying here.

She fell silent for a while. He thought she might have fallen asleep until a few minutes later the nurse stepped in and spoke softly.

"Yes?" the nurse said.

"She woke up. I gave her a little water answered a few questions for her, but she fell back to sleep." Snake kept his voice just a soft so he wouldn't wake Jenny.

"I'm not asleep. I can't sleep with that beeping. Can we shut off whatever it is?" Jenny didn't open her eyes, but her hand squeezed his as she spoke.

Snake didn't answer, but turned a questioning look to the nurse. The nurse, whose badge said her name was Brenda, took gloves from one of several boxes mounted to the wall and pulled them on as she stepped closer.

"I'm glad to see you awake. I can't turn the machine off completely, but I can mute it." She moved to one of the machines and tapped the screen, after a moment the sound stopped.

Snake was glad, the sound had been getting on his nerves, but he'd been doing his best to ignore it.

"Thank you." Jenny's voice was soft.

"Want more water?" Snake asked, ready to grab the cup, if she said yes.

"Not yet. I'd like to sit up a little bit, if I can, though."

Snake looked to Brenda for approval and at her nod, he reached for the button on the bed to lift the head.

"Tell me when to stop," he said, but kept his eyes on her face, watching for any sign of discomfort.

"There. That's good," Jenny said after it raised several inches. She started to lift her head and look around.

"No, stay leaning back. Conserve your energy. You've been out for several hours, and you'll be more tired than you think," Brenda said as she checked the machines around the bed and checked Jenny's vitals.

"When can I get out of here?" Jenny asked again, this time aiming the question at the nurse.

"Not soon enough to suit you, I'm sure. You took a pretty good blow to the head and had to have surgery, to relieve the pressure, but it looks like you should recover just fine. I'll let the doctor know you're awake. She'll come in and see you then we'll have a better idea of when they'll discharge you after that." Brenda kept her voice upbeat and cheerful, without actually giving any information. Brenda asked Jenny several questions, how she was feeling, about her pain levels, and a few more, that Jenny answered without hesitation, though she never pulled her hand from where it still sat woven with Snake's.

After a few minutes, Brenda left, saying she would let the doctor know Jenny was awake, and that the doctor may not make it around to see her until morning but if she needed anything, all she needed to do was hit the call button.

"How long was I out?" Jenny asked a few moments later. "When was the accident?"

"Between the surgery and the time after, you were out for somewhere between ten and twelve hours. The accident was this morning."

"What time is it now?" she turned her head as if looking for a clock or a window to get an idea of the time.

"It's late, almost ten."

"And you're still here? What about visiting hours?"

"We have a little pull here. Kinard's been here a long time. And I wasn't about to let you wake up all alone. Not after I screwed up and you were more hurt than I realized."

"You didn't have to do that." She closed her eyes and shook her head. "Did someone call Chuy? I don't want to mess up his honeymoon."

"Sadist called him. Told him you'd been in an accident but not how bad it was or that you had to have surgery. He just told him you are okay and that we have everything covered."

Jenny frowned, obviously not happy that they'd called her brother. "I wish you hadn't."

"We felt like he needed to know. Right now, he's waiting to hear back from us on whether or not you want him home. He wants to cut things short and race back to take care of you, and we'll let him if that's what you want. But if you're good with it, we will insist he stay, and the Souls will make sure you have everything you need."

"Even someone to hold my hand, it seems." She used the fingers still interwoven with his to squeeze his hand then relaxed again. "No. I don't want him home. I want him and Jill to enjoy their trip. They deserve this."

"I'll make sure Sadist knows to tell him you're good and to keep enjoying his time with Jill. We keep Gizmo too busy here for them to get much uninterrupted time while they're in town." He used the hand she wasn't holding to pull out his phone, then went to typing up a message to the club VP, who was acting as President while Tuck was in Wyoming, and let him know about Jenny and what she'd said. He glanced up at her and saw her eyes drooping. "You rest. I'll be here when you wake again."

"No, go home. Get some sleep. I'm fine." Jenny's words had started to slur, he wasn't sure if it was the pain medication or because she was drifting off to sleep, but no matter what she said, he wasn't going anywhere.

12

Jenny woke to find the room nearly dark. It must be either very late or very early, but she didn't see a clock, so she wasn't sure which. She blinked several times, trying to make her brain wake up enough to remember what woke her. It seemed to take longer than it should have, but she realized she needed to use the restroom. What had the nurse said about that? She couldn't remember, but she did remember she'd said to call if she needed anything.

Jenny looked around and spotted the red call button on the side of the bed beside her. It took a moment but was finally able to lift one hand and press the button. Soon the door pushed open and a woman who looked a few years older than her appeared.

"Do you need something?"

"I need to use the restroom but I'm not sure how to manage it." Jenny motioned to the IV in one arm and toward the foot of the bed as she still hadn't seen whatever was going on with her leg, only had Snake told her it was broken.

"You can get up and go to the bathroom, but you'll need help. Let me make it a little easier for you."

"Get her ready and I'll help her into the bathroom." A voice from the corner startled Jenny.

It took a moment to realize Snake had been sitting there and she hadn't even realized he was still in the room. Why hadn't he gone home like she'd told him to? She stared at him a moment, wondering that as the nurse came around the side of the bed and messed with the tubes and wires attached to her.

When she seemed satisfied with the tubes, she lowered one of the rails at the foot of the bed and hit the button to lower to the foot of the bed.

"I need you to take it slow. Swing your feet off the side and sit there for a moment. You may be dizzy, and we don't want you to fall, okay?"

Jenny nodded and pushed herself more upright, then shoved the blanket and sheet down toward her feet her legs came into view, one bare, the other wrapped in a puffy thing that looked like the air packing she sometimes got in the box when she ordered stuff online. She stared at it a minute, knowing she should feel something, but it looked like it belonged to someone else, not her and she couldn't make herself think of it as hers, at least not yet.

She swung both legs off the side of the bed and let them hang there as she braced her hands on either side of her hips. The nurse had been right. The world seemed to spin around her but slowly it stopped. The leg with the funny air thing around it ached a bit, but not enough to say anything about.

The nurse moved a walker in front of her.

"You need to use this. Don't put any weight on that leg. Not yet. If you don't think you can manage the walker, we'll get a wheelchair until you can manage the walker."

Jenny stared at the walker a moment then shook her head. "I can do it."

"We'll make it work. If I need to, I can carry her in there," Snake spoke up, reminding Jenny he was still there.

She looked up at him, but didn't know what to say so she turned her attention back to the walker.

"How's your head?" the nurse asked. "Are you dizzy at all?"

"No. I'm good now."

"Then slide off the bed and land on this foot." She gently touched the leg without the puffy thing on it.

Jenny nodded, then did as she was told. It took her a couple of tries, but she managed to get the hang of sliding the walker forward a few inches then putting her weight on her arms and hopping forward. The nurse went with her, staying on one side while Snake stuck close to her other side.

Pain shot up her injured leg with every hopping step, but she wasn't going to let it stop her. Something told her if Snake had any clue how bad this trip hurt, he would put a stop to it. She wasn't about to let that happen so Jenny clenched her teeth and continued.

When they reached the bathroom door, the nurse opened it and held it open while she continued inside at what felt like a snail's pace.

"Are you more comfortable with me helping you or him?" the nurse asked, keeping her gaze on Jenny.

Jenny looked at her, then at Snake then back to the nurse. Which would she rather have help her in the bathroom?

"He's fine." Jenny didn't know where the answer came from. Maybe instinct? Why else would she ask for a man she barely knew to help her do something so private? Not that she could change her mind because the nurse had already nodded and stepped back, letting the door swing shut, and leaving Jenny alone in the bathroom with Snake.

"Let's get you over there, then if you think you can handle it, I'll step out and let you take care of your business. When you're done, call out and I'll step back in and help. Don't try to do too much on your own. The last thing you need is to fall and hurt yourself more." He kept his tone businesslike and impersonal, helping her to keep from thinking too much about what was happening.

Jenny nodded and continued toward the toilet. When she got into place in front of the commode, he stopped before stepping out and used one finger to lift her chin until her gaze met his.

"I'm serious, baby. Do not push yourself. Do not do too much. You fall and hurt yourself more and Gizmo will come home early."

That threat alone was enough to make her have second thoughts about toughing it out and trying to get out of here on her own. She nodded her acceptance but didn't say anything else. She didn't know what to say.

He watched her face a moment longer then gave her a single nod, as if they understood each other, then left her to finish her business.

13

Snake stood outside the bathroom, watching the nurse move around the room, while he waited for Jenny to do what she needed to in the bathroom. He might not know her well, but he'd been able to tell from the stubborn set of her jaw that she wasn't going to ask for help when she was through with what she needed to do. That was why he'd made a point to tell her if she fell and complicated her injuries, then Gizmo would come home.

He hadn't lied to her either. It had taken some swift talking and more than a little reassurance from Sadist to keep Giz from hopping on a plane and coming straight back.

She hadn't said so, but from the look on her face, he didn't think she would be pushing the issue. A moment later he heard the toilet flush, but stayed where he was as he waited to see which won, her stubborn streak or her determination that her brother not be called home early.

Snake didn't have to wait more than a few seconds before he heard her call out.

"Okay, I'm ready." Her voice was muffled by the door but still clear enough to know what she was saying.

He didn't hesitate, but opened the door and closed the distance between them until he stood beside her.

"Do you need help standing?"

"I don't think so, but I didn't want to try it and fall."

"No problem. Go ahead and try. I'll let you do it, but if something goes wrong, I'm right here to catch you."

She nodded, put a hand on either side of the walker and slowly stood. He knew it couldn't be easy balancing on one foot even with the walker to lean on, but she didn't complain.

"Good job," he said once she made up right and stood still a moment as if trying to catch her breath. "Back to bed?"

"Not yet. I need to wash my hands."

"Okay." He stood by as she made her way to the sink, then stood behind her, refusing to look down at the gap in the back of her gown, and wrapped an arm around her waist to keep her from falling as she bobbled while washing her hands. He kept his arm in place as she dried them, then took several deep breaths.

Snake noticed the face she made at her reflection but kept silent about it, and about the beads of sweat popping out on her forehead. He wanted to swing her into his arms and carry her back to the bed, then tell her to stay put until she was well enough to get up again. But he knew enough about her, both from the time they'd spent together at the wedding and from the stories Gizmo told to know that wouldn't go over well. She was too independent for her own good.

Part of him wanted to do it anyway, then threaten to swat her ass when she protested, another part knew it was a bad idea. Instead, he waited until she'd regained her balance then released her waist and walked her back to the bed.

By the time Jenny was back in bed and the nurse satisfied with her tubes and wires, it was apparent the short trip had exhausted her.

"Talk to me about your pain levels," the nurse said once she was situated and seemingly comfortable.

Jenny glanced in his direction with what he thought was a guilty look.

"Don't try to sugar coat it because I'm here. That trip had to hurt, but you had to do it to learn that. Now tell her how bad it hurts and be honest." Snake tugged a chair closer to the bed so he could reach her once he was seated.

He listened while Jenny talked to the nurse and the nurse told her there were orders for pain meds and it wasn't too soon for her to have another dose.

He bit back the urge to tell the nurse not to let it go too long again, that there was no need for Jenny to hurt like that. He hated seeing her hurt, but knew better than to piss off the person who could make things more difficult for Jenny just by being a little less attentive. Not to mention she could get him thrown out.

After the medication had been fetched, taken and the nurse had left again, Jenny spoke to him for the first time since they came out of the bathroom.

"Why didn't you go home when I said to?"

"Because Gizmo wouldn't want you to be left alone." He didn't tell her how much he hated seeing her lying there so pale and still and that he couldn't bring himself to leave her like that. Instead, he reached over and covered her hand again, doing what little he could to comfort her. It only took seconds for her to weave her fingers in with his, but several minutes for her to start to relax. Nearly an hour passed before she could relax enough to go back to sleep.

14

It took another day and a half before the doctor would let her out of the hospital. By the time she'd signed all the paperwork, and they brought in the wheelchair she was ready to hobble out on one leg and the splint they'd velcroed her into a few hours before that went from her ankle nearly to her knee.

Life with that would be so much fun, she was sure. But at least it wasn't a fiberglass cast. She'd asked why not when they'd been getting her into the splint, and once they'd answered, it seemed obvious. This made it easier to get to the incision and keep it clean not to mention see any signs of infection before it went too far. Jenny wasn't sure if it hadn't occurred to her because she was tired or if the pain meds were making her brain foggy. She didn't think it was a side effect of the other surgery they'd done. They small hole that had been drilled into her skull to relieve the pressure from a subdural hematoma. There had been a lot of explanation on how they often didn't catch them until later when they were more severe, she had heard some of it but most of it drifted over her head. She hoped it was because of the pain meds. What mattered though was that she had a small wound near her hairline where they'd inserted a tube to drain things. Still, she didn't think that was what was making her fuzzy.

But that didn't matter now. She was free, or nearly. And that was all she could think about at the moment. Well, that and the burly guy walking beside her down the hall. She didn't think he'd left her since the first time she'd woken in the hospital. At least he'd been there every time she was awake. And she couldn't figure out why.

It wasn't that she wasn't grateful not to have to go through it alone, she was. And it wasn't that she didn't like him. She did. Maybe a little too much. But she barely knew him. Why would he spend days in the hospital if he didn't have to?

Maybe that was it. Maybe someone had ordered him to stay with her, to make sure she was all right and didn't get into any more trouble. That she could believe.

Except he'd been nice. Sweet even. And if someone was doing something against his will, like sit in the hospital with a near stranger, wouldn't they at least be a bit sullen or put out?

She didn't know what he was thinking, his expression was blank, or if it wasn't she didn't know how to read his expressions, so it might as well be.

Jenny wished for a moment as the nurse wheeled her out to the loading area where a newer model sedan sat that she'd let them call Chuy home. She wanted nothing more than to sit down beside him, his arm wrapped around her as he told her everything would be all right.

Beth, the wife of one of her brother's friends, she couldn't remember which, came around and opened the back seat door.

"This will be more room for you with that brace. We'll get you home and comfortable so you can heal."

That sounded like the best thing Jenny had heard all day. What she really wanted was a soak in a tub full of hot water, but that would have to wait. She couldn't do that for several weeks, at least until after the incision where they'd fixed her leg healed.

"I'll be glad to get settled, take something and at least have my own things around me." Jenny made the awkward transfer from the wheelchair into the car, sliding her butt all the way across the seat so she could rest the brace in the seat. The seat belt was a little uncomfortable this way but still functional.

After they got her settled into the car, Beth came around and got into the driver's seat.

"Are you sure you don't want us to call Gizmo back? He'd want to be here, I'm sure." Beth glanced at her in the rear-view mirror before turning her gaze back to the road.

"I'm sure. He's only going to get one honeymoon. I don't want to ruin it. Besides, once I get home, I'll be okay. I can sleep and start feeling better in my own space." Jenny closed her eyes and let her head fall back against the seat. She didn't need to watch traffic, after her last car trip and what had happened since, it only stressed her out. Plus, she didn't want to think about replacing her car. That was something else she'd have to do, sooner rather than later.

Had anyone contacted her insurance company? She bit back the urge to groan as the list of things she needed to do grew, and still, all she wanted to do was sleep in a comfortable bed.

Before Jenny knew it, Beth pulled the car into a parking area, stopped, and killed the engine. Jenny picked up her head and looked around. This wasn't her apartment complex.

She frowned as she tried to figure out where they were. She didn't recognize the warehouse they were parked in front of or what looked like a mechanic shop on the other side of the car. The door in front of her opened, revealing Snake.

"Will it be easier to come out this way or back out the other side?" he asked.

"Why is my car here?" Her frown turned to a scowl of confusion.

"Because I brought it here. Which way out of the car?"

Jenny turned back to him and shook her head as if trying to clear it.

"Why did you bring it here?"

"So, Mac can take a look at it. If anyone can fix it, he can. Unless you want it totaled?"

She frowned again, trying to track the change of subject that left her painkiller addled brain just a little slow.

"Why am I here? I thought I was going home."

"Sorry about that. Sadist didn't like the idea of taking you home to be alone. He decided to bring you here, at least until Gizmo gets back. That way we can make sure you have everything you need," Beth said from where she stood behind the open door watching her with apprehension.

"What I need is my own bed and my own things," Jenny muttered, but she couldn't argue that it would be nice not to have to worry about how to get to the bathroom or fix dinner. She took a deep breath and let it out in a rush before looking back to Snake. "What was it you asked?"

"Do you think it will be easier to get out of there forward through this door or backward through that one?" he motioned to the door behind her.

Jenny considered the question for the first time, looking at the door, then her leg, then back at Snake through the doorway.

"I think backwards will hurt less, but I'm not sure how well it will work."

"Let me worry about that." He disappeared. She assumed he was going to get someone to help.

"I'm sorry about misleading you," Beth said from where she still stood behind the open door. "I didn't know how to tell you I wasn't taking you home. Not when you seemed so set on it."

That didn't make sense to Jenny, but she wasn't sure if it was because of how Beth had said it or that her own brain wasn't working right. The door behind her opened, startling Jenny. She started to fall backwards, but only went a couple of inches before the door stopped her. She sat up and turned to see Snake standing there.

"Ready now?" he asked.

Jenny leaned away from the door, and he pulled it open.

"I'm going to grip you under the arms and tug. When you can, get your good leg under you. Don't worry about falling. I've got you until you can get that leg out, okay?" He waited until she nodded to touch her, then his hands were gentle as they lifted and tugged her out of the car.

As soon as she could, Jenny let her good leg drop to the ground and pushed enough so she stood on it, even though her injured leg was still propped up on the seat in the car.

"Good. Beth come around here, please?" Snake called even as he stopped pulling on her. He released his hold under her arms and instead stood beside her, one arm wrapped around her waist as if he was snuggling in close, not just keeping her from falling.

She liked having him there. It felt right. And he smelled amazing. She didn't know if it was cologne or just the scent of him, but it made things low in her belly stir and heat.

"What do you need?" Beth asked as she reached them.

"Can you ease her leg down. I don't want to let it fall on its own. That would hurt, a lot, and I didn't want to leave her to stand like a flamingo while I did it myself," he said from where he still held her up.

Jenny looked around, wondering where they were, obviously not her place but where was this? And who else was here? She didn't have long to wait. Once Beth eased her foot off the seat of the car and down till it hung next to her other leg, Snake spoke again.

"I'm going to help you inside. We'll get you a pair of crutches so you can get around more easily on your own, but until we do, someone will be around to help you. You ready?"

Jenny frowned again as she wondered who else would be around, but nodded as the weight of her leg started to make her hip throb.

"Give me a sec," Snake said as he kept an arm around her but moved around so he stood next to her injured leg. "Ok, lean your weight on me like I'm a crutch and we'll go inside."

She shot him a look that she hoped expressed her skepticism about how well that work, but did as he asked anyway, leaning against him as she made a hop with her good leg. When her foot hit the ground, she clenched her teeth at the bolt of pain that shot up her injured leg and through her entire body, but she couldn't stop the inhaled breath that became a hiss between her clenched teeth.

"I was afraid of that, but I wanted to try it this way because I thought you'd be more comfortable with it." Snake's words barely penetrated the haze of pain that was slowly receding from her brain. Before she had time to register what he meant, he'd bent and scooped her up into his arms.

A moment of panic at the sudden shift made her wrap her arms around his neck as she tried to keep from falling, though trepidation flashed through her as she knew she would be too heavy for him to carry for long.

"You don't need to do this," she said, her face buried against his chest.

"How else are we going to get you inside? Think about how bad one step hurt, walking a couple hundred yards will only be worse. This is small and something I can do. Let me." His voice vibrated through his chest and her whole body, sending sparks of heat through her, despite the throb in her leg and her feelings of guilt that he was carrying her.

Before she knew what was going on, he bent and eased her down into a chair. Reluctantly, she released her hold on his neck so he could stand. She looked around while he propped her braced leg up on another chair with a pillow that seemed to materialize out of nowhere.

"There you are, at least for a few minutes. We're still working on getting a room ready for you. Krissi was running a little late this morning, but she's here now." Beth seemed to be rambling, but Jenny wasn't about to stop her, she was too busy taking in the room where Snake had deposited her.

"Can we get you anything? Are you hungry? I know hospital food leaves something to be desired. We can get you something much better here, or something to drink if you'd like?" Beth seemed eager to do anything she wanted.

Jenny wasn't sure if this was good or bad.

"Food would be good. What do you have?"

"There are a lot of options really. What kind of food to you feel like?"

"What sounds the best is beef enchiladas, or a cheeseburger and fries."

"Anything to drink?" Beth asked.

Jenny turned toward the bar along one wall to see what they had.

"No alcohol. Not with the pain meds they've got you on," Snake put in from where he'd sat down in another chair once he'd finished making sure she was comfortable.

Jenny shot him a frown then turned back to the bar.

"A soda would be great."

"Coke or Pepsi, we've got both."

"Got any Mountain Dew?"

"We do. I'll get that for you." Beth hurried off, leaving Jenny blinking after, and wondering what next.

15

Snake watched as Jenny discussed food with Beth and seemed to take in the clubhouse. He knew she'd never been here before and had to be brimming with questions, but she didn't ask. He couldn't help but wonder what made her not ask.

"Tell me how you're feeling," he invited.

Jenny turned to watch him for several seconds, then blinked and shook her head as if clearing it before speaking.

"Not bad. My leg aches a little but not enough to worry about."

He hated that she hurt, but knew it was too soon for more pain meds. He hated that he couldn't just make the pain stop.

"I know you wanted to go home, but we didn't want you there alone."

She nodded, but didn't say anything, instead, kept looking around with wide eyes. He glanced around the room, trying to see it as she might, as someone who had never been here and probably never into an MC hang out before.

There wasn't a huge amount to cause alarm, at least not at this hour. Well, maybe the stripper pole in the corner where the couches and TVs hung on the wall. But at least it was empty. The rest of the place looked much like a bar in a warehouse might. Though most bars didn't have a second floor. Not that there was more bar or anything too wild up there. Now he thought about his room upstairs and that as soon as he had a chance, and Jenny was settled in, he'd have to stop by his house and pick up everything he'd need to spend at least a week, if not more here. He liked having his own space back, but he was still more comfortable here. That was part of why he'd volunteered to stay on site while Jenny was here, to make sure she had all the help she needed.

Not that her being here would keep him from working most days, as the prospects would be around if she needed anything. Still, he couldn't help but wish he could be here for her any time she wanted or needing anything. Where the hell had that thought come from? It wasn't like him, but he had other things to occupy his thoughts right now, so he pushed the idea from his mind and turned his attention back to Jenny.

"There are rooms upstairs, we'll get you set up in one then you can take a nap or whatever you'd like. Is there anything I can bring you from your place to make you more comfortable?"

She mugged a face that made him realize maybe she didn't want some guy she'd known only a few days to go rooting through her apartment.

"Or we could ask one of the women to go, if that would make you more comfortable?" He hoped that hadn't sounded as pleading and desperate to her as it did to himself. Still, he hated seeing her hurting like this and wanted to do everything he could to make it better.

"There are a few things I'd like. I'll make a list, though I'm not sure where my purse is, or my keys, so I don't know how they'll get in."

"I have your keys. They were in the car when I brought it back, so I pulled them out for when you'd want them. I think your purse is in the bag with your things from the hospital. If it's not there, I'll check the car for you. You have your phone, right?"

"I do. But it's dead. Has been for a while and I didn't have a charger in the hospital."

"What kind of phone is it? I'll see if we can locate a charger for you."

"It's an android. Type C charger," she said without bothering to pull it out.

Snake smiled; he could just bring her down one of the cords from his room. "I think we can find one of those. You do know that normally it's Gizmo we'd go to for that kind of thing."

Jenny lifted one corner of her mouth in a wry smile. "Yeah, I know. He's my go to too." She took a deep breath, then grimaced before letting it out slowly, as if the movement had made something hurt, or hurt more.

"What is it?"

"Nothing, just sore ribs. I know better than to breathe that deep, but I forget and keep doing it."

Savage came around with a large stein filled with ice and Mountain Dew and set it on the table in front of Jenny.

"Your food will be out soon. Let me know if there's anything else I can get for you."

"Just one thing right now." She tilted her head up to look at the prospect.

"What's that?"

"What's your name?"

"Savage, ma'am."

"Enough with the ma'am stuff. I know I've never been around much, or ever, if I'm being honest, but I know a few names and I'm trying to match them to faces. I'll learn the rest of you too before too long."

"No worries. You can call out for me or wave. I'll keep an eye out in case you need anything."

"Thank you," she said.

Snake watched as the prospect went back behind the counter, leaving the two of them alone. Jenny picked up the big cup and took a drink. She closed her eyes for a moment, and Snake couldn't help but wonder what she was thinking.

After a moment, and another sip, she set the mug back on the table and turned to look at him.

"So do you live here or what?" She watched him as if he were the only person in the room.

"I've got a house, but I only recently got back into it."

"Were you having work done?" she asked, a frown creasing her brow.

Snake wanted to tug her into his arms, to smooth that crease away and make sure she didn't have anything to worry about. Where the hell had that thought come from?

"No, I was out of town for a while, working. I leased it out while I was gone. No point in letting it sit empty. When I came back, I had to wait for the lease to run out." He lifted one shoulder in a dismissive gesture. "It wasn't too bad. I got a room here and I was good."

The crease in her brow deepened for a moment. He thought she was going to say something else, but Savage appeared carrying two plates. He set the plate of enchiladas in front of Jenny and the other just to the side of it.

"Beth said you couldn't be sure which you wanted, but you hadn't had good food in a couple days, so I made both. Eat whatever looks good to you. I hope you start feeling better." The kid shot her a hopeful smile, then left, heading back to the kitchen. Snake assumed to clean up whatever mess he'd made cooking.

"I can't eat all this." Jenny looked back and forth from one plate to the other, as if wishing she could.

"No worries, eat what you want, I'll take what's left," Snake said.

She twisted around and stared at him with wide eyes, as if she couldn't believe what she'd heard. "Really? Chuy used to do that for me, but why would you?"

"Why not? I know the food here's good, I mean I lived here for a few months, I should know. Besides, it will make you feel better, and it's small thing to do."

She looked at him for a moment as if not sure he was being serious, then turned back to the plates in front of her. She stared at them for a moment then looked back to him.

"Would you mind if I had the enchiladas and some of the fries too?"

"Not at all. Help yourself." He motioned to the plates with one hand.

She slid the plate with the burger on it around until it was in front of him, then tugged hers closer and picked up her fork. Snake watched her for a moment then picked up the burger and got started.

He didn't know how long he would be hanging around the clubhouse, but if most of that time was like today, he wouldn't be complaining.

16

Jenny finished her plate of enchiladas, and about half of the fries on Snake's, plate, trailing them through the left-over sauce on her own plate before eating them. After she was done, she looked around, wondering about the room for her that Snake had mentioned before, and where it might be.

Hadn't he said the rooms were upstairs? How on earth would she get up and down the stairs when she couldn't even walk?

She wished they'd just taken her home. At least there she didn't have to worry about a flight of what looked like rickety metal stairs so she could take a nap.

Beth appeared, a baby in her arms, one Jenny was almost certain didn't belong to her.

"Your room is ready, whenever you are ready to go up. You'll be in room five." She bounced back and forth as she spoke, jostling the baby who cooed in her arms.

"Thank you. Is this the baby from the wedding the other night? I don't remember her name." Jenny fought the urge to reach out and tickle the little one's toes.

"It is, and her name is Ashley. Her mama is upstairs finishing up a couple things and I thought I'd take advantage and get some time in, plus, let Krissi work without having to worry about her." Beth grinned at the baby then over to Jenny. "Want to hold her?"

"I don't know if I should. What will her mother think? What if she cries?" She didn't remember the last time she'd held a baby, though she and Chuy had too many cousins for it to have been never.

"Krissi won't think much of it. And Ashley is used to being passed around. Most of the club has a hand in raising her and as I'm sure there will be more babies around, and sooner rather than later if the rate the guys have been finding partners is any indication, she'll have plenty of playmates too. Here."

Beth handed the baby to Jenny, who panicked for just a moment, but when Ashley smiled and gurgled as she stared up at the new face, Jenny's heart melted and she couldn't help smiling back, no matter how tired she was or how much she'd been dreading attacking those stairs to get to her temporary room.

With her attention on the baby in her arms, Jenny didn't know how much time had passed until Ashley yawned, triggering one of her own. She blinked several times and Ashley laid her head against Jenny's chest and closed her eyes. Jenny watched her, wishing she could do the same. Find a nice warm body to curl up against and just take a nice, refreshing nap. But since she broke up with her last boyfriend more than three months ago, and Chuy was out of town, and now spent more time with Jill than with Jenny, that wouldn't be happening, at least not any time soon.

"Come on over here, sweet thing." An unfamiliar, deep voice pulled Jenny's attention back to the present.

At the same time, the sweet weight of the baby against her chest disappeared as a man she thought she remembered as the girl's daddy lifted her from Jenny's arms.

"What's your mama gotten up to?" He settled the squirming girl against his own chest and turned his attention to Jenny. "You're Gizmo's sister, right? I met you at the wedding. I'm Ruger."

She liked that he didn't assume she would remember him among the myriad of names and faces she'd seen that night.

"I remember seeing you. That's a sweetheart you have there."

"I know." He glanced down at the baby now snuggling against his chest, swiftly drifting off to sleep. "I'm sorry you got hurt, and I respect your decision to let Gizmo enjoy his honeymoon, but that means we're all going to step up and make sure you have what you need. Sorry if that means you can't be home where I'm sure you'd rather be. Bear with us though, we'll do our best to keep you comfortable, at least until Gizmo gets home and you can argue with him." The man kept a pleasant expression as he told her in a nice way that she wouldn't be going home soon.

"I'm coming to terms with it. We've got an extended family, but Chuy and I haven't been close with them for a long time. I guess I got used to it being just the two of us. And I got used to doing a lot for myself when he was busy."

"It's not the two of you anymore, and hasn't been for a long time, but I guess you didn't know that. You do now." He gave her a kind smile, then continued, "It looks like you're as tired as my princess here." He turned to look at Snake. "Why don't you take her up to her room so she can rest, make sure she knows how to call for help if she needs anything." Ruger looked back to Jenny. "We'll have some crutches here before dinner time, so you'll have at least a little mobility on your own."

"That sounds great." She didn't say that she didn't know how she'd manage the stairs, even with crutches, there was no point right now. Maybe by the time they came time, she'd have figured out how to do it.

"Are you ready to go up to your room?" Snake asked from where he still sat at the table with her.

She looked up at the railing that hid what she was sure was a row of doors heading into what was likely dorm-like rooms, then back to him. She wasn't looking forward to that trip, but she was exhausted, and a nap sounded heavenly. She just hoped the bed was more comfortable than the one in the hospital had been.

"Yeah, might as well."

"I know you're not looking forward to the trip. I'll make it as easy for you as I can."

"It's not me I'm worried about. I mean I know I'm no featherweight, it won't be easy to carry me up those stairs."

"Let me worry about that." Snake stood. "Ready?" He scooped her up and carried her to the stairs and up.

When they reached the top, he didn't pause before taking her to the door with a small 5 on it and pushing the door open.

"Do you need the restroom first?" he asked, not even winded from carrying her.

How did he do that?

"I should. That way I won't have to get help to go before I lay down again."

"No problem." He carried her through a door she hadn't noticed, and set her on her foot in front of the sink. "Do you need help? I can get one of the women if you'd be more comfortable with them."

"I can manage from here, if you'll give me a few minutes?" She smiled as she dropped the hint, hoping he would take it and she wouldn't have to tell him outright to leave her alone for a few minutes.

"I'll be in the bedroom. If you need help, just call out."

"Will do." She didn't say that the only way she'd call for help before she was done was if she fell and broke her other leg, he'd never leave if she admitted that. Instead, she smiled and watched as he turned and left, pulling the door closed behind himself.

She braced herself on the edge of the countertop and the wall to maneuver around the room to take care of her business and wash her hands afterwards, then she hobbled over to the door and opened it.

Snake stood from where he'd been sitting in one of the two chairs next to a table she hadn't noticed on her brief trip through the room.

"You were supposed to call me." He rushed forward to help her.

"I managed on my own just fine and I need to know if I can make it to the bathroom on my own or if I'll have to call for help every time I need to pee."

He scowled as he tried to help her to the bed. Jenny wanted to evade him and hop over on her own, but she didn't want to make her leg hurt even more than the dull ache that was already bothering her, so she let him help her.

Once she had settled on top of the bed, he stepped back and looked around the room.

"Is there anything else I can get for you?"

"You were going to find me a charger for my phone," she reminded him. She leaned to one side so she could wiggle the device from her pocket. She stared at it for a moment, wondering what good it would do, as the thing was dead. At least she was more comfortable with it out of her pocket.

"That's right. I'll be right back." He turned and left.

She blinked, wondering where he would find one, then shook her head and looked around the room. Taking it in for the first time. It wasn't quite the dorm style room she'd expected, but it was close. And this was the first time she'd seen a dorm style room with its own bathroom. Not to mention a bed this big, it was at least a queen, maybe even a king size. Then there was the TV mounted to the wall at the foot of the bed. Maybe having to stay here wouldn't be so bad.

Before she had a chance to decide if she wanted to take a nap or turn on the TV, Snake was back. He knocked twice on the door he'd only pulled close and not quite shut then pushed it open.

"I've got that charger, let me get it set up for you. I also brought a notebook so you can make a list of whatever you want from your place. We'll send someone over to gather it up for you." He came over to the table beside the bed, bent down, shifted the table a bit, then a moment later held out a cord. "Here. Oh, here's your phone. I'll just plug it in." He did, then straightened and stepped back. "There's a phone next to the bed, or you can use your cell, I wrote several numbers in the notebook, you can call or text any of them if you need anything. I work next door at the mechanic shop so I'm around all day if you need anything from me. Savage or another prospect will be around all day, you can call them too. All the numbers are on the list."

She nodded, not sure she would remember this, but she'd try.

"I'm going to let you rest a while, someone will come up and check on you after a while or you can call someone if you need something before someone comes up."

"All right." She set the notebook beside her phone, she'd add the numbers in once her phone was charged. Now though, she'd decided between watching TV and a nap, it hadn't been the TV to win.

"Don't hesitate to call if you need anything." He shot her a scowl before backing out of the room and closing the door.

Jenny took a deep breath and let it out, enjoying being alone for the first time since leaving the hospital. It took her a few minutes to inch herself down the bed until she was laying, then a few more to get comfortable, but she managed it, without any help.

As she lay there, relaxing, she hoped Chuy was having a good time on his honeymoon. He deserved every bit of happiness he could get. He'd always been there for her when she needed it, this seemed like a small thing she could do for him, to let him have this trip.

As long as no one let it slip how bad her injuries were.

17

A fter leaving Jenny to rest, Snake made his way back down to the main room of the clubhouse. He looked around wondering what everyone was up to, but nothing interesting caught his eye. He should go to the shop and see if he could get in a couple hours' work. If nothing else, so he didn't feel so restless, but should he leave her? He turned and looked at the railing her door, and his, sat behind, and decided she was likely napping anyway. She wouldn't need him for a couple of hours, at least.

Without giving him time to second guess the decision, he headed for the door, then across the parking lot to Mac's. In one bay was a truck needing an oil change. That was something he could do with his eyes closed. After a brief chat with Mac to let him know that he was here and ready to work, Snake pulled on a pair of overalls and got started.

He'd finished the oil change and moved on to another job, this time changing out a set of spark plugs. After a while, Snake was glad he was working on routine things that would normally bore him out of his mind. Today, for some reason, he couldn't manage to get Jenny off his mind. He found himself wondering how she was doing, had she woken yet? Had she called someone for help? Was whoever she called helping her? Why hadn't he heard from her?

At least working on routine jobs, it was harder to lose track of where he was and what needed to be done next as his mind wandered. He finished that job and moved onto another, glad that Mac seemed to notice his distraction and had assigned him a third maintenance job, another oil change. He'd pulled the drain plug and was using the time while the oil drained to grab a drink when Mac approached him again.

"Finish this one up and call it a day," Mac said, then turned to move on to the next man.

A glance at the clock told Snake it was nearly six and time for the shop to close. Surprise flashed through him. He hadn't been aware of that much time passing, but now that he thought about it, and the work he'd finished, he wasn't surprised. But, again, he couldn't help but wonder how Jenny was doing and why she hadn't at least texted him. With a shake of his head, he tossed the empty cup he'd been drinking water from and went back to work. The faster he finished the job, the sooner he could go check on her.

After cleaning up as best he could in the shop sink, Snake made his way back to the clubhouse, he asked Savage for a water and if he'd heard anything from Jenny.

"A couple of the women went up and sat with her a while, then they left together, said she was napping again, and they were going to her place. They haven't come back yet, and I haven't heard anything from her," the prospect said before moving to the other end of the bar where another Soul was trying to get his attention.

Snake didn't like that the women, whichever ones they'd been, hadn't come back yet, or that Jenny hadn't at least called down for more food. He headed for the stairs, intent on going up to check on her, but before he could set foot on the first step, Sadist called his name.

Snake bit back a curse, changed direction and headed for the club VP.

"What's up?" he asked as he approached the table where Sadist sat.

"Have a seat." Sadist motioned to one of the other chairs around the table.

This didn't bode well for the discussion. Snake suspected he was about to be given an assignment he didn't want. Right now, that meant any assignment that would keep him away from Jenny. He told himself he was just worried about her and being a good brother to Gizmo, taking care of his sister until Giz returned. He hadn't yet convinced himself, but he was trying. He pulled out a seat and sat, not wanting to piss of the man in charge before he had to, and Sadist was in charge while Tuck was still in Wyoming, though the time he was due to come home was getting closer and closer.

"You've spent the most time with Gizmo's sister, I think. Tell me what you think of her."

This was so unexpected, Snake didn't know where to start.

"She seems like good people, just like Gizmo." The last thing he was going to tell his VP was that he found himself thinking about her at the oddest times. Nor was he going to tell him the direction some of those thoughts had taken. They definitely weren't thoughts you should be having about a brother's sister.

Sadist lifted one brow but kept watching him, as if expecting more. Snake lifted one shoulder and let it drop.

"I spent a couple hours with her during the rehearsal and the reception, since then most of the time I've spent with her as been while she was unconscious. I barely know her."

Sadist continued to watch him as if he knew there was more that Snake wasn't saying. There was but it wasn't anything the club needed to know, at least not yet, and nothing that would impact club dealings. It was personal.

"I want to know more about her," Sadist said after a couple minutes. "Especially with her staying here at the clubhouse." He lifted one hand in a stop gesture to keep Snake from protesting. "I'm not saying I don't want her here. I ordered it. I think it's best, especially if she continues to insist on not telling Gizmo the truth about her injuries." Sadist shook his head. "As much as Beth disagrees with me on that, I have to admire her for that decision. She is determined to not take him away from this time with Jill, and that's good. She's thinking about someone other than herself, even when she's this hurt. It's a good trait." He took a deep breath, glanced up at the second-floor railing and exhaled slowly.

"What I don't know is her politics. Her loyalty and if she can be trusted. Right now, nearly everyone in the building can be trusted with what we have going on." Sadist shook his head as the ghost of a smile curved his lips. "We haven't had any hookers around here in a while. At least not any who hung around for more than a night or two. Not since shortly after Double D pissed off my wife. I guess she didn't like the way Beth treated her. She must have talked to the others and decided the Souls clubhouse wasn't the place to pick up any random ride.

"Anyway, I need to know how much we need to guard what we say, how careful we need to be. We've got a few things going on and I need to know if I need to steer men around the clubhouse or if we can still use this place as headquarters."

Snake eyed the other man for a few moments, trying to decide if that was all there was to it or if Sadist had something else on his mind, something he wasn't telling Snake. He didn't think so and if there was, Sadist wouldn't give it away.

"I'll see what I can find out. Savage said some of the women went up and spent some time with her, then were headed to her place, but haven't come back yet. You know anything about that?"

"Yeah, it was Krissi, Beth, and Elyse. They would have been back by now, but something came up with Ashley. I didn't catch what exactly, only that it wasn't serious, and would only cost them a bit of a time delay." He looked across the room at the clock over the bar. "They should be back soon. Why don't you go up and check on Jenny, see if she wants to come down for a bit, maybe have some dinner. Maybe the girls will be back with her things by then."

Even though he hadn't said as much, Snake knew Sadist had just dismissed him, and reminded him that he wanted him to spend more time with Jenny. Not that Snake found that to be a hardship. The more time he spent with her, the more he wanted to spend. There was something about her that not only did he like, but he found her appealing and relaxing in a way he couldn't say he'd experienced with many women.

Standing, he pushed his chair back where it had been then went upstairs to see how Jenny was doing.

18

Jenny woke and stretched, wishing for at least the tenth time today that the brace on her right leg wasn't so heavy. She lay staring at the ceiling, wondering what time it was and how long she'd slept this time. A look around told her it was still light out, so it couldn't be too late.

Her stomach rumbled, reminding her that she'd spent a day and a half in the hospital with nothing decent to eat, and though the meal she'd had when she'd gotten here had been delicious, it seemed to have been a long time ago now. She should see about calling someone for help to get more. But before that she needed to use the restroom. Jenny hated calling someone in to help her go the few steps to the bathroom.

Maybe she could make it herself?

It took her several minutes of struggling, but she managed to sit upright and swing both legs off the edge of the bed. She sat there trying to catch her breath when a soft knock sounded on the door.

Thinking it was the women who had been here before, Krissi, Beth, and Elyse, back with her things, she didn't bother asking before calling out.

"Come in." She didn't bother to lift her head from where she was sitting, breathing in and out as she tried to move past the bolt of pain that had shot through her at moving her leg.

"What are you doing?"

Snake's voice made her jump and look up, hoping she didn't look guilty.

"Sitting up." Jenny did her best to keep a blank expression, hoping he wouldn't rip her a new one.

"And obviously trying to get up by yourself." He pushed the door closed behind him as he hurried to her side. "Why didn't you call? I would have come to help you. For that matter, there are nearly a dozen men downstairs who wouldn't hesitate to help you either."

"I know." She looked away. "I just feel like an idiot needing help to go a few feet to the bathroom. You said someone would bring crutches tonight?" She hoped that would distract him from what she'd been trying to do.

He moved to her side and without asking scooped her up off the side of the bed and carried her into the bathroom where he set her on her foot and held onto her while she braced herself on the edge of the sink.

"I'll be in the bedroom when you're done." He left her to take care of her business without another word of reproof.

She went about her business, taking a little extra time to wet one of the washcloths she found on the shelf and wash her face before hobbling back to the door and opening it. Snake sat in the same chair he'd been sitting in hours before when she'd opened the very same door. This time he didn't scowl or chew her out. Instead, he looked up from his phone as if he'd been entertaining himself while he waited.

"You ready to go down and get something for dinner? I just checked in with Kinard, we'll have the crutches here for you in an hour or so. Krissi and the others were supposed to pick them up while they were out, but something happened with Ashley, and they haven't made it that far yet."

"Oh no! I hope she's all right."

"Sadist assured me no one is hurt, it's just some baby thing." He shrugged, clearly having no idea what could have happened.

"As long as everyone is good. Sure, I'd like to get something to eat. But I hate to ask anyone to come get me. But please don't think I've been sitting up here all alone because I didn't want to ask for help. I have only been awake maybe twenty minutes."

"I'm not judging. If you want to sit up here all alone, that's up to you. I would like it if you'd stop resisting asking for help. That's why we brought you here instead of your place, so you would have help."

"I get that. And I appreciate it." She started to take a step from the bathroom doorway toward the bed, but the bolt of pain that shot up her injured leg made her stop and only clenching her teeth kept her from crying out.

Snake stood and hurried to her side, bracing her side and helping her to the bed.

"I haven't even turned my phone on yet. I was talking to the girls the first time I woke up, then I just woke up and was trying to get to the bathroom. I'd like to get my phone and go downstairs if you don't mind."

"I'm happy to take you down when you're ready. Are you comfortable? I'd ask if you want to change clothes, but your things haven't gotten here yet." He stepped back once he'd gotten her to the bed.

She thought it was to give her a little space, to decide what she wanted to do. Jenny stretched over to the table and picked up her phone.

"We can go downstairs whenever you're ready," she said as she looked for a pocket to put her phone in but the scrubs they'd given her at the hospital, and cut up the side of one leg to accommodate her brace didn't seem to have any pockets.

"Just hold it. Or if you want to try to walk, I can carry it for you." He stood a couple of feet away, waiting until she was ready.

"I'm not going to even try to walk. Moving around and going to the bathroom hurt enough." Jenny shifted, trying to get more comfortable.

"You ready?"

"Whenever you are. Though I'm still not sure you should be carrying me around. You're going to end up hurt. I'm too heavy."

He picked her up and swung her into his arms, ignoring the comment about her being too heavy.

"Can you grab the door?" he asked as he stepped up to the still closed door.

She used one arm around his neck in case she slipped, the last thing she wanted to do was fall, then opened the door with her other hand before dropping her phone into her lap and using both arms to hold on.

She managed to keep from burying her face in his chest as he walked along the hallway to the stairs, but once he started down, she couldn't take it anymore, and hid her face so she didn't have to see the ground approaching. She kept it there until they reached the ground.

"Where do you want to sit?" Snake asked, pausing at the base of the steps.

She looked around then nodded to one side of the room. "Can I sit there? I can rest my leg on the bench instead of on another chair."

"Sure." He carried her over and got her situated, then stood. "If you're okay here, I've got a couple guys I need to talk to. I'll be here somewhere, and I'll be back to check on you."

"I'm fine. Do what you need to." She looked around the room, trying to see who all was here and if she recognized any of the others.

The blond they called Sadist sat a few tables away talking to a couple men. There were several others clustered in twos or threes around the room talking. There were also a few women, but no one she recognized, and a little girl, well, not that little.

She looked maybe fourteen or fifteen. She sat sideways on the lap of a man who was obviously several years older, but not old enough to be her father.

Jenny blinked and tried not to stare. She'd known that some of these clubs didn't always care about the law, but she was surprised Chuy would put up with something like that. He'd always been super protective about girls being taken advantage of by men. Maybe it wasn't what it seemed? Or maybe he'd never seen it. She forced herself to look away.

"What can I get for you?" the same guy who'd brought her food this afternoon asked.

What had his name been again, Savage?

"Can I get a Mountain Dew to start, and do you guys have a menu or is there anything special ready tonight?"

"No problem on the soda. No menu, we have mostly an expanded bar food type thing available, but if there's something special you want, ask. I'll try to see if we can put it together. As for specials, we don't normally have them, but one of the old ladies brought in a huge pan of lasagna this afternoon."

"Oh, that sounds amazing. Can I get some of that too?"

"Sure thing. Give me just a few minutes and I'll be back."

"No worries. I'm not going anywhere." She motioned to the leg that had her stationary, at least for a while.

Savage gave her a weak smile, then went back to the bar, and through the door behind it. Jenny picked up her phone and powered it on. Might as well see what kind of messages were waiting for her.

19

S nake kept an eye on Jenny as he talked to a couple of his brothers. First, he cornered Sackett, who often worked the bar, though Savage had been on that duty today. He made sure the prospect, as he hadn't yet been given his patch, knew who Jenny was and how she was to be treated, then he went in search of Maverick. He hadn't spent much time with Mav since they'd gotten back from Texas, not that he'd spent a huge amount of time with him while they'd been there, but they'd been there together and that was a bond he only had with a couple of other men. It hadn't helped that Maverick had met his old lady before Snake had made it back to town.

Bubba had made it back around the same time he had, and he'd had his woman with him too, though he'd made the trip to Alabama to rescue her from some messed up shit. Bubba was still getting Sissy used to the brothers, so they came around but more often than not he didn't bring her. She was coming in more often though and that was a good sign.

The front door opened, drawing his attention. Krissi stepped in looking a little harried, Ashley in one arm and a diaper bag slung over the other. Behind her was Elyse, carrying a collapsable playpen and something else.

Before the third of the group, Beth, could make it through the door, Snake was headed to help. Even if they had all the baby stuff handled, there would be Jenny's things to bring in and up to her room.

I t was a little after nine when he noticed Jenny sitting at the table where he'd left her earlier, yawning. She was still surrounded by some of the women of the club, though different ones had come and gone all evening. He'd checked on her several times, making sure she had everything she needed, but resisting the urge to hover.

He made his excuses to Crash and Dumbass and made his way over to the table.

"You doing okay? You want to head upstairs?"

She turned and looked at him for a moment, her expression confused. He didn't know if it was exhaustion, medication, or something else but she looked like something wasn't right.

"I'll make sure you make it if you want to try taking the stairs with your crutches." He motioned to where the assistive devices were leaning against the bench she sat on.

She blinked then shook her head as if clearing it.

"I'm sorry. I guess I'm more tired than I realized. Where did you come from?"

"I was just over there." He motioned to the far side of the room where he'd been talking to some of his brothers.

She glanced in that direction, then turned back to him.

"Yeah, I think I'm ready for bed." Jenny turned back to the rest of the ladies at her table. "Sorry. I'm just exhausted. Will I see you again soon?"

"Any time you like, just give one of us a call," Amber said. "You can get our numbers from your guy there." Crash's woman tilted her head in Snake's direction.

He ignored it, he wasn't going to delay Jenny getting some rest to set her straight on something that didn't matter anyway.

Snake stepped back out of the way and watched as Jenny made her way to her feet, looked for a pocket to stick her phone in, then gave up and held it out to him. He took it without a word and shoved it in his pocket as she picked up the crutches and started for the stairs.

While he loved to see that she was independent and wanted to do things for herself, he hated to see her hurting or in pain and he knew from experience that the harder she pushed now, the longer she would be hurting. He also knew her well enough already to know telling her that would do no good. It was something she, and most people, had to learn on their own.

When she made it to the base of the stairs, he stayed a couple steps behind, waiting to see if she wanted help, or if she was going to try it on her own. His relief was palatable when she stopped, stacked both crutches together and turned for him.

Snake took the crutches and leaned them against the outside of the stairs.

"I'll get those once you're upstairs," he said as he scooped her up and started up the stairs. Once more she wrapped her arms around his neck as if she was afraid he'd drop her, but this time she didn't bury her face in his chest. Oddly, he found he missed it. "You need the restroom?" he asked as he stepped into her room.

"No, I went a little bit ago."

"No problem." He set her down on the bed. "I'll be right back with your crutches. Is there anything else you want from downstairs?"

Jenny shook her head, and he went to retrieve her things.

"Where do you want these?" he asked when he returned with them.

"How about there?" She pointed to the table beside the bed. "That way I can reach them when I'm ready to get up."

He leaned the crutches against the table.

"Anything else I can get you?"

"No. You've done so much already. I don't know how to thank you for everything."

Jenny looked so down, so lonely that Snake didn't even try to resist the urge as he sat on the edge of the bed and cupped her cheek.

"It will be okay. We'll make sure of it. We'll take care of you until Gizmo gets home, and even after. There's no need to be so down." He used his thumb to wipe away the single tear that trailed down her cheek.

She sniffed. "I know. I'm just, I don't know what. I shouldn't feel like this. There's no reason to, but I can't seem to stop it."

"Aww, sweetheart. Is there anything I can do?" Snake didn't know what made him ask that but now that it was out, there was no way he could take it back.

She was quiet for a moment, and he thought maybe she was going to tell him no, when obviously she needed something, someone. His stomach roiled at the idea that it would be anyone else, but he stayed quiet, waiting for her to say something.

"Would you mind staying with me for a while? Just a little while." She seemed in a hurry to reassure him she wouldn't monopolize him for long.

"Sure. Where do you want me?"

Jenny looked up at him through spiked lashes. "Would you mind sitting up here, next to me?" She patted the bed beside her.

"Not at all. Let me get my boots off so I don't get your bed all filthy." He went to one of the chairs and toed off his boots before moving around to the far side of the bed and sitting with his back against the wall, much like she was doing. He lifted one arm and wrapped it around her shoulders, encouraging her to lean into him. He hoped being close and held would help her feel better.

Jenny leaned over and laid her head against his chest. The tension seemed to drain from her slowly. After a while he rubbed her back, then smoothed one hand down the length of her hair.

Snake thought she might have fallen asleep and wondered how he could get up and let her rest without waking her up. Then she moved. She brought her hands up to cover her face and he realized she wasn't sleeping, she was silently crying.

His chest ached at the idea she'd been here leaning on him, silently crying. He didn't know what to do other than to let her cry, let her get it out, and to be there. So he continued as he had been, smoothing his hand down her hair, gently rubbing her back, but he added soft reassuring sounds and words.

"It's okay, sweetheart. Everything will be okay." He didn't try to stop her from crying or reason her out of it. He figured she'd been through a lot in the last few days, and she'd taken it well. There was no doubt she needed to let out all her pent-up emotions. So, he did what he could, he was there for her and there to comfort her when she was done.

Snake didn't know how long she laid against him crying, and he didn't care. There was nowhere else he needed to be, at least not for a long time, and oddly, nowhere else he wanted to be.

20

Jenny realized she'd been leaning on Snake, crying for more than half an hour. She was mortified. There was no way she would have done this if she'd thought about it but that was the thing. She hadn't thought about it. She'd been so tired, so lonely, even with people all around her, then he'd been so nice and asked if she needed anything.

It had been impossible to resist the urge to ask him to stay. And once he'd agreed to stay, he'd been so nice. It hadn't taken long for everything to just get to be too much.

She'd done her best to keep him from knowing she was crying. But it hadn't worked. To her surprise though, he hadn't freaked out like Chuy usually did. Snake hadn't tried to get her to stop, making all kinds of wild promises and outlandish predictions the way her brother did. Though the memory of his reaction did make her smile. Instead, Snake had let her cry. He'd been soothing and comforting, but he'd let her get it out, and that was what she'd really needed.

"I'm sorry," she said when she was able to compose herself again.

"For what?"

He didn't seem fazed that she'd just cried all over him, and that confused her. No man she'd ever known would have thought nothing of something like that.

"That I broke down like that. I don't know what came over me."

"You've been through a lot in the last few days, sweetheart. I'd be surprised if it hadn't come out sometime. I'm just happy you feel comfortable enough with me to let it."

She wanted to look up at his face to try and gauge how honest he was being with her, but didn't want him to see how red and puffy her face got when she cried, especially for more than a few minutes. Besides, she was comfortable, more comfortable than she'd been in days. She didn't know if it was that she was out of the hospital or that he was here, and at the moment, she didn't care enough to worry about it. Instead, she closed her eyes and relaxed into him, wondering if maybe Snake was too good to be true.

W hen Jenny opened her eyes, it took her a moment to realize she must have fallen asleep. That she was still curled up against Snake didn't make things easier, but in some ways it did. Had he fallen asleep too? Was he just sitting there holding her to be nice? She hoped not. It couldn't be comfortable for him to sit there all night like this.

Heat pooled low in her belly, and she wished she had the courage to wake him up with a kiss. But that wasn't her. What if he said no or pushed her away? She shifted, trying not to disturb him in case he was asleep.

"You all right?" His voice was soft, but dispelled the thought that he might be sleeping.

"I'm good. I need to use the restroom though." She sat up and turned, swinging the brace off the edge then her good leg. She sat for a moment making sure she didn't get dizzy as she sometimes did when taking pain meds. "How long was I asleep?"

"Not long, maybe an hour."

"You should have woken me. You didn't need to stay." She reached for the crutches, braced herself and stood. Snake didn't respond, but she felt his eyes on her as she made her way to the bathroom.

When she opened the door after she'd finished, she found Snake sitting in the chair, stepping into his boots. Though she'd expected him to leave now that she wasn't being so pitiful, a pang of disappointment shot through her.

"I've got a meeting I've got to attend downstairs. I don't know how long it will take. Probably not more than an hour. Would you like me to stop by when I'm done?"

"Sure, if you don't mind." She tried to keep her face blank so he wouldn't see how much she hated the idea of him leaving or how much better it felt that he'd offered to come check on her again.

Maybe she was more to him than just a favor to a fellow club member. She pushed down that hope and made her way to the other side of the table where he sat. When he'd brought her things up earlier, he'd set them on the table, and she hadn't taken the time to go through them, figure out what was here and neaten them up, maybe stack them on top of the dresser. She didn't know whose room she'd taken over, but she didn't want to be too nosey and get into their things. Now would be the perfect time for that.

"You need anything to drink or anything else before I head into the meeting?"

Jenny shook her head. "If I need something while you're gone. I'll call downstairs. I promise."

"Try one of the women, Savage or Sackett, the rest will be in the meeting too."

"Okay." She opened the first bag and saw it was clothes, which wasn't what she was after right now and she didn't want to unpack her underwear with him in the room, so she opened the second bag. That one had her laptop and e-reader. She was glad to see them. She tossed them onto the bed and closed the bag to set them aside. She could do that tomorrow. Now she wanted to check a few things online, things she hated to do on her phone because of the smaller screen, then maybe settle in and read for a bit. That couldn't tire her too much, could it?

Snake watched her a moment longer, then leaned over and dropped a soft kiss on top of her head.

"I'll see you in a bit." He cupped her face tilting her head up until she looked him in the face then he brushed a soft kiss across her lips.

The whisper of a touch was gone before she could decide how to react, but the feeling of his mouth against hers, his fingers against her skin and the fissions of heat both sent through her body lingered long after he'd left.

21

"We've got a shipment coming through next week, I'm going to need some men on that." Sadist scanned the room as he spoke. "You'll take the merchandise to the Utah border, so plan to be gone at least a day, probably overnight. I'll let you know exactly who will be going in a couple days."

Murmurs spread across the room but quickly quieted as Sadist shifted in his seat, plainly not through talking.

Snake watched his brothers, mentally noting reactions and who said what.

"On to other business, prospects. How many of you have met Boomer?"

Snake scanned the room and found about half the men had raised a hand, including him, though they all remained silent.

"Good. Not bad, so far. I'm not going to ask what you think. It's too soon for that. What I do want to know is if any of you have any negative encounters with him, or anything to stop him from going forward with the club." Sadist scanned the room as he waited for anyone to speak up.

Again, no one spoke.

"That's good," Sadist continued after a moment. "We should have Sackett's new Kutte ready before then. I thought we might give it to him, then send him on the ride, then maybe we'll hold off on the patching party until after Gizmo gets home. It's not ideal, but I don't want to wait that long to give him his patches. Any objections?" He looked around the table but there were none.

Snake didn't know how he felt about it. On one hand he was glad the party would wait, he wasn't sure he was ready for something like that while Jenny was in the clubhouse, but he didn't want her excluded either. Maybe her spending more time around the club and his brothers would settle that, whether she chose to be a bigger part of the club or walk away entirely.

Just the thought of her walking away entirely made him want to hit things, but he did his best to hide it. This wasn't the time or the place to do that or even get into it.

"Now, on to prospects, we're down to Savage and boomer here, and Malice up north. I've had several leads I've been working on for a while. It looks like things are finally happening. We should have one new prospect by the end of the week, and another by the end of the month. We are running the backgrounds of any prospects up north but they're handling the prospect period and voting in themselves." He fell silent for the span of several breaths, letting the news move around the room and giving the men a chance to calm back down. "The first is Puck. I'm not sure when he'll be here yet, other than by the end of the week. I'll let you all know when I know more. The second goes by Demon. I've got a bit of information, but more will be forthcoming." Sadist's gaze landed on Snake. "Snake, I'd like to talk to you for a few minutes after we dismiss, if you don't mind."

Snake nodded. He knew that if he didn't mind was just to be polite, if he refused the meeting there would be hell to pay.

Sadist talked business for a few more minutes, Snake followed along, but didn't pay much attention. His mind had once more drifted back to Jenny, and he couldn't help wondering if she'd fallen asleep waiting for him. He felt bad that she was lonely and wanted him of all people, who would have thought he would be any woman's choice, for any reason.

He didn't feel like he had much to offer her, well, other than maybe a shoulder to lean on. But any of the others could offer her the same, and often, more.

Sadist called the meeting to an end while Snake was lost in his own thoughts. It was only as the door opened and many of his brothers filed their way from the back room where meetings were held that Snake realized what was going on. He stayed where he was because the VP had asked to speak with him. While he waited, Snake noticed that Ruger hadn't stayed, neither had Maverick who was acting as Sergeant at Arms, at least until Ghost came back from Wyoming. *If* Ghost came back from Wyoming. Snake wasn't sure if the other officers leaving was a good thing or a bad one. He couldn't help but wonder what it was Sadist wanted to talk to him about, at least he wouldn't have long to wait.

When it was just the two of them in the room, Snake stood, closed the door as he assumed this was private or Sadist would have approached him in the main room rather than asking him to stay after the club meeting, and went to sit closer to the VP.

"Thanks for staying. I have a favor to ask."

Relief washed through Snake, it wasn't anything awful. Well. Maybe. He'd spent two years in south Texas as a favor to the club. While that was something that had needed doing, it wasn't something he wanted to repeat any time soon.

"All right?" Snake kept his tone careful. He didn't want to volunteer too soon, in case it was another mission like the last. He had been gone too long and hadn't been home long enough to suit him. Plus, he didn't want to leave Jenny, at least not until Gizmo returned.

"You're sticking close to the club house to make sure Jenny is taken care of, what I'm hoping is that you'll be around when Puck arrives, keep an eye out for him, and when he does arrive, show him around."

"Like I did for Boomer?" Relief made Snake want to slump in his chair, but he didn't let it show, instead he made sure he was clear on what the VP wanted from him.

"Pretty much, yeah."

"Not a problem." He leaned back in his seat and watched the club's temporary leader for a few seconds. "Honestly, I thought you were going to give me a mission like the one in Texas. I was trying to think of a way to refuse that wouldn't piss you off."

"You don't want another mission like that?"

"I'm not going to say never again, but I will say it's too soon. I need to spend some time here, remember what real life is like, before I'm ready to go out on another extended mission like that."

"Then there's Jenny."

Snake shook his head. "That's only temporary. Gizmo will be home before too long then I won't feel like I need to stick close to her."

Sadist didn't reply, just watched Snake for several seconds, one brow lifted. The longer the other man watched him, that look on his face, the more Snake wanted to shift in his seat.

"Is that all, you just want me to keep an eye out for the new guy? Show him around when he gets here?"

"That's my only favor. I did want to offer a bit of warning though."

A ball of dread formed in Snake's stomach. "About?"

"Jenny."

"What about her?" Snake clenched his jaw in an effort not to jump to her defense. He needed to hear what the warning was first.

"Keep in mind she's a brother's sister. Things go bad with her, it could lead to bad blood with Gizmo, and the last thing any of us wants is bad blood with our tech guru. Our lives depend on him, remember that."

"I won't forget who or what she is, and as for Giz, I love him like a brother, you know that, but he's not our only guru anymore or we wouldn't have been able to let him go for two weeks for a honeymoon. You know that as well as I do." He held up one hand stopping Sadist before he could argue. "Not that I'm going to do anything stupid. I'm not screwing around with Jenny just to screw around. I'm trying to be a good brother to my brother, and there for to her."

"Are you trying to tell me that you see her like a sister?" Sadist's expression made it clear he didn't believe that.

Fuck, even Snake didn't believe that.

"No, I'm saying I'm trying to treat her as I would a sister. Make sure she's taken care of and has what she needs, at least until Gizmo gets back." After that, he'd do his best to keep his distance to keep anything that shouldn't from happening. He had ideas about what he would like, but he wasn't going to push her into anything.

"You keep trying to tell yourself that." Sadist leaned back in his chair, watching Snake. "Anyway, that was all. You can go do whatever you have planned for after the meeting. I'm going to find Beth and see what she has in mind." He stood, pushing his chair back as he went then left, leaving the door open on his way out.

22

Jenny couldn't help but wonder what this meeting Snake had to go to was about. Since he'd not mentioned leaving, and had said all the other brothers, except the two she knew were prospects, would be busy, she assumed it was downstairs and club business. Gizmo hadn't said much about that, only enough to know she shouldn't ask once he returned. Still, she couldn't help but wonder.

When her laptop popped up a low battery alert, she stared at the bag she'd pulled it from and tried to remember if she'd seen the power cord. She thought she had but she'd have to get up to retrieve it then find somewhere to plug it in. A quick look around didn't reveal an electric outlet to plug into but Then she remembered Snake moving the table next to her to plug in the cord for her phone. There was no way she could do that on her own, not right now. So she closed the computer and set it on the table, telling herself she'd ask for his help later, and picked up her e-reader. She settled on something to read then laid back and quickly got lost in the story.

"Jenny?" Snake's voice was soft. "You still awake?"

"I am."

He stepped inside, closing the door behind him.

"You found your computer. Good."

"I did, but I need help to find a plug in." She picked up the cord and showed him the plug. "I'm afraid even if I'd located one, I wouldn't have been able to get to it."

He looked at her a moment. "You want it plugged in over there or over here at the table?"

She thought about it a moment. "Over there is good. I think the cord is in that bag." She pointed to the bag she'd pulled the computer from.

"Let me see," he found the cord in the bag, looked under the table, found an outlet, and plugged it in.

"Thanks." She set her e-reader down to sit up then reached for her crutches. "I need to use the restroom really quick. You won't leave while I'm gone?"

"Go. I'll be here when you come back." He took a seat at the table while she shuffled into the bathroom.

When she returned, he sat in the same chair, seemingly content to wait.

"What's the plan for tonight?" she asked as she made her way back to the table.

"I didn't have one. Other than making sure you don't need anything that is."

"Need? No, I've got everything I need, at least for now." She fell silent and wondered if she should say anything more.

"But?" he asked, seeming to know she had something on her mind.

Jenny took a deep breath and let it out slowly, trying to figure out who to put her thoughts into words.

"I'm worried." That seemed the simplest way.

"About?"

There it was. He'd asked the hard question.

"It might be easier to say what I'm not worried about." She sighed, then continued, "About work, about my car, about Chuy, about you, about the Demented Souls, about my place. And that's just off the top of my head."

"You seem to have a lot on your mind. Let's see if I can help you break it down a little. Make it a little less intimidating."

She frowned and tilted her head as she looked at him. "What do you mean?"

"I mean if we break down each of your concerns, talk about it some, we might make them less of a concern and take the issue off your mind."

She stopped at the table and grabbed her phone as she passed by and tossed it onto the bed before continuing on the crutches. "Oh, that reminds me, before I forget. Is there wi-fi here and can I get the password?"

"Yes, there is wi-fi, but I don't remember the password. I'll have to ask. Normally I'd go to your brother but if you ask him, it will be a giveaway that you're more injured than we let on to him. You can ask Krissi though. She would know."

"Oh, good to know. Thanks for telling me." She made it to the bed, sat, leaned her crutches against the side of the table, then swung her brace up onto the bed before picking up her phone and sending a message to Krissi about the wi-fi password. "Are you going to come sit with me?" She arched a brow in his direction hoping he would take it as her expecting to be obeyed in this.

He took a deep breath and let it out in a rush. "Give me a second." He toed off his boots and made his way to the other side of the bed in his stocking feet. "I'm not sure this is a good idea," he said as he sat beside her, his back to the headboard and legs stretched out in front of him.

"I don't know why it wouldn't be. We're both adults, besides all that's happening is we're talking."

"Tell me more about what's on your mind. You said you are worried about work. What about it?" He seemed to be ignoring her comment that they were both adults, along with the rest of it and moving on to what he'd suggested earlier.

She took a deep breath and rolled her shoulders. "I don't want to lose my job, but I can't work like this." She used one hand to motion to the leg that was still encased in a brace from above her knee to her ankle.

"You've called them right, to let them know you were in an accident and hurt? What did they say?"

"I did call in, that first day from the hospital. They said get better, don't worry about it, but I can't help it. This is going to have me out for a couple weeks at least. What if they get tired of waiting and find someone new?"

"How long have you been there?"

"Almost two years."

"Surely in two years you can't be the only one who's gotten hurt or sick and had to be out for more than a day or two."

She tried to remember if anyone had been out more than a couple days at a time in the whole time she'd been there. At first, she couldn't recall anyone then she did.

"There was one, her mom was sick and in the hospital for several weeks, then she passed away. She ended up taking like four weeks off; if I remember right."

"And did they replace her?"

"No, I mean they had a temp come in from the lab, but when she came back her position was waiting for her."

"Why would they do any less for you?"

His tone and argument were so reasonable it made her feel silly for even thinking about it, but she couldn't help what her brain said to her.

"I don't know. I just worry about it."

"Well, the next time it comes to mind, remind yourself, they didn't let her go, and they won't let you go. You can't help this, you'll be fine." Snake reached over and laid a hand on top of hers, smoothing his thumb back and forth over the back of her hand in a motion that made her stop clenching it in the leg of the scrubs she still wore. "What was the next thing on your list of worries?"

Jenny tilted her head back and let it rest against the wall as she tried to remember the list she'd given him of the things she worried about.

"I think my car was next."

"What about your car are you worried about?"

"I'm worried I won't be able to fix it. I'm still making payments and I need the car to get back and forth to work. I have to warn you, this one often circles back and has me worrying about work again."

"I can see why it might, but let's try to talk it out. You said you're worried you won't be able to fix it. I already told you that if it can be fixed, Mac can do it. But let's go to the worst case and get that out of the way. You're still making payments, I assume that means you have insurance, right?"

"Of course."

"And when you bought it, did you get the gap insurance?"

"Yeah. Someone told me it's a good bet, probably Chuy."

"Then even if you can't fix it, the insurance will pay it off. You might have to find another car and maybe start out with a new loan, but we can help you with that."

"Okay, you're right, that's not that bad."

"And that's all worst case scenario. That accident wasn't your fault, and the other driver's insurance will end up paying out. And if they give you trouble, which I'll admit is likely, and you may have to get an attorney, but that means they'll also sue for pain and suffering compensation. That will mostly go to pay the attorney, unless you find one with killer rates. But still that will mean you end up with more than just a replacement car and your bills paid. This is a significant injury and will mean significant medical bills. Unless things have changed, they use the medical bills as part of the formula to figure the payout. By the time it's done you may be able to not just replace your car, but upgrade it."

His thumb still worked back and forth over the back of her hand. She liked it and didn't want it to stop, even as she wanted to feel his hands elsewhere.

"I guess you're right. But how long will it take to replace it if I have to do that? How will I get to work? What if I can't? Then I'll lose my job for sure."

"That one's pretty easy. We have loaners we use at the shop. We can make sure you have transportation, even if I have to pick you up every day and take you to work and back home at the end of the day. We'll make sure you're okay, sweetheart. We're not going to let anything happen."

His words were reassuring, but she ached to be held, to have someone hold her close and tell her they would take care of it all. Not that she would ever let someone take care of all her worries, she just wanted someone to want to.

"Okay, I'll try to stop worrying about it. I don't know if I'll be able to manage it, but I'll try." She relaxed some, leaning over and laying her head on his shoulder. Jenny liked the way he felt and the way he made her feel, as if her worries were valid, not stupid or like it was stupid that her brain would hyper focus on these things with her permission. She loved that he was willing to help her think them through, so they weren't so much of an issue.

23

"Now that we've worked out the job and your car, what was the next thing on your list?" Snake resisted the urge to wrap his arm around her and pull her closer. He loved that she trusted him like this.

"I think the next thing on the list was Chuy."

"Why are you worried about your brother?"

"You'll think I'm being stupid."

Snake frowned as her voice dropped to little more than a whisper. "No, I won't. I promise. It's worrying you so I will take it as seriously as you do."

"I'm worried that now that he's married, he won't have time for me. That he won't care when I need him." She turned and buried her face against his shoulder as if even voicing her concerns out loud embarrassed her.

Snake gave up the fight not to wrap his arms around her and hold her close. She obviously needed it. He wrapped one arm around her shoulders, and shifted her, carefully so as not to jostle her leg, so she sat between his thighs, letting her curl into his chest if she wanted to. He held her for several seconds as he tried to figure out how to say what needed to be said.

"Number one. Gizmo is your brother, and that is never going to change. He's going to be there when you need him, no matter who else is in his life. Number two, has he not been there while he was dating or engaged to Jill? Why would that change now?"

"I know. I never said my worries were rational, just that I was worried. I am worried, even if I know they're stupid worries. I can't help it."

"Hey," he smoothed one hand up and down her back, "I never said they were stupid or irrational. I'm trying to give you things to think of when they become too much. You can't always help what you think about or what you worry about, but you can arm yourself with some arguments, some things to counter what your brain tells you. I'm not saying it will be easy but with work it will get easier. Tell me more about your worries. I know you mentioned me in there. What are you worried about with me?" His chest ached as he thought about how she was feeling and how she probably had even more unfounded worries about him. All he could do was work with her, to offer her things to remind herself when things came to her mind.

She took a deep breath and let it out slowly as if trying to regain her composure. "Are you sure you want to know, it's kind of dumb."

"None of your fears are dumb, sweetheart. And yes, I want to know. I can't help you battle them if I don't know what you're worried about." He wondered who had told her that the things she worried about were dumb or stupid. Where had she gotten that idea? If he did nothing else, he would help her see that her concerns and worries were valid, even if you knew better. It kept you sharp. She just needed to learn to address the ones that weren't helping her in some way and to let go of them.

After several moments, where he thought she was gathering her courage to share her worries about him, she spoke.

"I'm worried you're just here because of Chuy. I'm worried you see me as an obligation that you can't wait to be rid of. I'm worried that you don't feel the same way about me that I'm feeling about you." She barely moved her face from where it was buried in his chest. Because of that and the way it muffled her voice, it took him a moment to register all that she'd said, and another moment or two to figure out how to address it.

"I can't deny that at first, I was here because of your brother. But that was only at first. While you were still in the hospital, something changed for me. It would be a lot easier for us both if it hadn't, or if I could keep this to myself, but you asked, and I won't lie to you. I don't see you as an obligation. That I can be one hundred percent clear on. As to the other part, whether or not I feel the same about you as you do about me, well, that's harder to answer. Especially since you haven't said how you feel." He continued smoothing his hand up and down her back, not willing to give up even that little bit of soothing her, and hoping it would help.

"That's part of the problem," she said, her face still buried against his chest. "I'm not sure how I feel. It's all so mixed up and confusing."

"What part is confusing?" Snake kept his tone gentle and calming as he questioned her.

"All of it." She took a shaky breath and he thought she'd fallen silent again but after a moment she spoke, "I hurt. I'm scared, those are pretty easy. But I'm also lonely, I want my brother, but I don't, and I know that sounds dumb, but it's the truth. Even I don't understand it."

"Then let's break it down a little more, see if maybe we can make it understandable. I think its two different things. You want him and you don't, and then you're lonely. First, tell me why you want him?" He wasn't questioning that she would want her brother when she was hurt and things were uncertain, he just wanted her to think about things, to break them down. Maybe that would help her understand what was going on and to deal with them better.

She took another deep breath, this time she seemed to hold it a few seconds before letting it out slowly, as if she was trying to focus on his questions, to come up with a real answer.

"Chuy has always been there for me, no matter what was going on, I knew I could lean on him. I think that's the reason I want him now, so I have someone to lean on."

"Good. Now tell me why you don't want him here."

"That one's easier." Some of the tension left her body, she relaxed more into him, leaning on him more than just burying her face against his chest. "He's on his honeymoon. I want him to enjoy this time. I want him to know I don't need him here all the time to take care of me and I can do at least a few things on my own. I don't want him to think I can't spend time without him and that I need him all the time, yet I miss him. I miss telling him about my day and his telling me it will work out. I guess in a lot of ways, Chuy has been like a dad to me. He's a stand in for whatever I need. I need to let go of that."

"I wouldn't say that, not entirely. He'd kick my ass if I encouraged you to let go of him. But we're not here making decisions, we're talking about your feelings and reasoning them out. That is all."

"Why though?"

"Why what?"

"Why reason things out if we're not making decisions?"

"Because reasoning things out, knowing why you're thinking things, and logical arguments, will help you combat the worries more on your own when you need to. Let's keep going though. You said lonely, but when I asked why it all revolves around your brother, are you truly lonely or is it just missing him?"

She was quiet a moment, and Snake assumed she was thinking about the question, trying to evaluate what she was feeling, so he remained silent, but continued running his hand up and down her back.

"I think I miss him more than I'm actually lonely," she said after several seconds. "I haven't had a chance to get lonely since the accident. I think the only time I've spent truly alone was while I was sleeping or in the bathroom. Otherwise, someone is always nearby, trying to make sure I have everything I need or want."

"Tell me how you feel about that."

Jenny picked up her head and looked up at his face for a long moment before she laid her head on his chest, face turned to one side. "It's a little overwhelming sometimes but it's sweet. I'm grateful for all you and the Demented Souls have done for me."

Her mention of the Souls reminded him she'd included the club in the things she was worried about. There were a lot of reasons to worry about the Souls for a lot of people, but she wasn't one of them. He couldn't help but wonder what about him and his brothers worried her.

"Now that you've brought up the Souls again, I want to skip a little bit and ask why you're worried about the club. I'll come back to the bit about you and me in a bit."

She lay still for the span of several breaths, then with a voice so soft he could barely hear her, she spoke, "I don't know what kind of club you are, and I don't know what kind of debt I'm incurring, nor what I'll have to do to pay it off."

Snake didn't know if he could be more surprised.

"First of all, there is no debt. We are taking care of you because you are Gizmo's sister. We would do the same for the family of any of our brothers. Since there's no debt, there's no need to pay one off, or worry about that. As for what kind of club we are, what kind of club do you think your brother would get involved in?"

He had to tread carefully here. It wasn't that the Souls didn't break laws or do illegal things, but they did them with what they all considered the greater good in mind. They all found that in order to get the evidence needed to get some of the worst people out there off the streets, someone had to get their hands dirty. And while yes, they sometimes made a profit on the things they had to do to make the world a safer place, they used that money to finance their operations. If Snake hadn't been convinced that what they were doing was to make the world a better place, then he wouldn't have spent two years in Texas trying, and succeeding, to gather enough evidence to get the leader of one of the largest cartels, responsible for countless deaths, both directly and indirectly through the poison he trafficked in, out of power.

"I thought I knew once, but there's so much he keeps secret. He won't tell me anything." Her voice was so lost, he wanted to hold on tight and reassure her that the club was a good one, made up of nothing but good guys, but he couldn't. They cultivated an image on purpose and if Gizmo hadn't confided in her, he couldn't, at least not yet. Maybe not ever.

"Sweetheart, you know your brother. Trust him, trust your instincts. If you have a hard time with that, try thinking about it this way, does Jill seem like the kind of woman who would be involved with the kind of thing you're worried about? What about Krissi? Beth? Elyse? Any of the other women?" Snake didn't know what else to say to reassure her. His chest ached as he wondered if his not being able to reassure her that the Souls weren't a criminal club would make any differencein what she possibly felt for him. It didn't make a difference in what he was beginning to feel for her, but what exactly was that? If she didn't want to look at it closer, he certainly wasn't going to push the issue. Why open himself up for heartbreak? Why give her that much power over him?

He didn't know how much time had passed before she answered.

"I don't know what the Demented Souls are into, but I know it can't be all it appears. You're right. Chuy wouldn't be part of the club if you were what you seem to be." She fell silent for a few more breaths, then spoke again, "I'll have to let that be enough for me, at least until someone sees fit to tell me more, if they ever do."

Snake kept his hand moving up and down her back, he wanted to tell her, but he couldn't. He didn't know her well enough to know if he could trust her with the club's secrets. To know if he could trust her with the lives of his brothers.

"I don't know what else I can tell you about the club to ease your mind. We're decent men. We are doing this because we consider you family, and you won't have to pay us back for any of it."

"Thank you. It helps, even knowing that much." She stayed where she was, but she seemed to be waiting for something.

"You said you were worried about your place. In what way?" Did she mean her place here, this room, her place in the club or even her home? There was too much left unknown to have any idea where to start with that one.

"Some of it is baseless, I know. Some of it we've already been over, it's just my own insecurities coming up and trying to bite me in the ass."

"Tell me anyway. Even if you know better, sometimes sharing the load helps. Even if nothing is decided or changed."

"I don't know if it will help, but I guess it can't hurt." She squirmed, as if trying to get more comfortable. He let her shift and waited for her to continue.

"Part of it has already been addressed."

"Tell me about it anyway."

"Okay, if you're sure you want to hear the way my brain works. Personally, I think it might scare you off."

"Sweetheart, do I seem like the kind to scare off easy? Hell, if the thought of what Gizmo will do when he finds out about this right here didn't scare me off, I'm not sure anything will."

"What do you mean? We're not doing anything."

"I know we're not and you know we're not, but I've already been asked if I know what I'm doing messing with a brother's little sister. Think about it. I spend a lot of time alone in a room with you. I'm even in your bed with you, even if we're not doing anything lascivious."

She picked up her head and scowled at him for a moment. "I'm not sure it works that way. Chuy wouldn't be upset with you just for being here with me." She shook her head as if she didn't understand and it didn't matter. She laid her head back on his chest and continued speaking. "My thought process on my place. Try to follow, I know it's a little convoluted." She let one finger play along the skin of his arm as she talked. It took everything he had not to tell her to stop. It tickled and he wanted to rub his hand over the skin to erase the feather light sensation, but he didn't want her to stop touching him. Though he could wish she would find a different way to do it.

"I'm afraid of losing my place. I worked hard to get a place of my own and I guess I'm a little insecure about keeping it. When I think about taking this time off work, that leads to thoughts of losing my job, that almost always leads to how long can I afford my place if I lose my job. Then what will I do if I lose my place? Where will I go?"

"Okay, let's look at that a little more closely. We already determined you're not going to lose your job, so we'll let that part go, but let's look at it from a little different angle. Do you have sick time? Disability insurance?"

She nodded, her head still resting against his chest. "I haven't taken more than two or three days of sick time since I started. And on the insurance, I didn't know if I should, but I thought better off with it and not need it than to need it and not have it. Besides, it doesn't cost very much a payday to keep it."

"Good plan. We need to figure out what needs to be done to file for them, but we can worry about that tomorrow or another day. And just for the record, worrying about if you have the money to keep your home, isn't complicated or odd, especially when something huge comes up like this accident. It's normal actually, at least where I come from. But from what I can see, you've done well in planning for emergencies. Better than a lot of people your age."

"My age. You sound like you're eons older than I am. Or that I'm a kid."

"I don't mean it to sound like that. I know we're not that far apart in age, what five or six years?"

"Something like that. I'm not sure I ever asked how old you are."

He watched her for a moment, wondering where this had come from and trying to remember if age had ever come up. He didn't think so. He'd always assumed she was younger than Gizmo, but was she really?

"I'm twenty-nine, if it matters."

"It doesn't, not really. And just for the record, I was right. You're six years older than me, roughly. I'm twenty-three."

"I know. You told me at the wedding, remember? I'm glad it's not too much, at least not enough to make what I'm feeling for you weird."

"That seems so long ago, even though it's only been a few days." She shook her head. "Since you brought it up again, what is it you feel for me, exactly?"

Something fluttered in his stomach. Was he really ready to admit this? What if she didn't return his feelings? No. She'd asked and she was worried he wouldn't feel the same. He suspected they'd find that they had similar feelings for each other, the real question was how would her brother take it?

24

Butterflies fluttered in Jenny's stomach as the conversation turned to the topic that had her the most upset earlier, well other than the possibility of losing her job.

"A lot more than I should for a brother's little sister, I'll tell you that. Things I should keep to myself and not act on. But damned if I can help myself."

"What do you mean?"

He didn't answer, instead used one finger under her chin to tilt her head up until she looked at him.

"Tell me to stop if you don't want this." His words whispered along her cheek as he lowered his face to hers and slowly, sweetly kissed her.

Jenny found herself stretching closer, her fingers curling into the soft cotton of his shirt as she tried to get closer. Snake's hands smoothed down her body and tugged her closer. The kiss turned hotter than she'd imagined it could be causing her to lose track of time or any sense of the outside world. Everything ceased to exist except the two of them and the heat between them.

When he pulled away, Jenny couldn't stop the whimper of loss that escaped from her throat. She wanted more. A lot more.

"Does that tell you what I'm feeling?" His voice had dropped an octave and the deep timbre rumbling along her inflamed senses, made her want to pull him back to her for another searing kiss, and more.

"It does. It tells me we're on the same page. But why did you stop?"

"Because you're hurt. You're tired and I don't want to push you for more than you're ready for. We can take our time and make sure when we do come together, it's good for both of us."

"I don't want to wait. I am okay. I can handle it." She didn't want to stop. Her whole body throbbed for release, and she knew just who she wanted to give it to her.

"I have no doubt you can handle it, but I don't want to risk accidentally hurting you." His hand smoothed down her back again, she loved having his hands on her, but she wanted to lose the layers of cloth between them.

She took a deep breath and let it out as she relaxed against him. "Can you at least stay with me? I'm tired of lying alone in a room or even having someone to one side in a chair. I want to have you close if I can."

"I can stay, but don't push for sex. I am serious about this. You need to heal before we go there."

She couldn't help rolling her hips as the heat pooled between her thighs at the mention of sex.

"Damn. I really want some but if you're adamant, I guess I can be good." She closed her eyes and relaxed into him, listening to his heartbeat and absorbing the feel of his body against hers.

"How about you get ready to lay down, I'll go change and grab a couple things, then we can go to bed if you want. Are you tired?"

"I shouldn't be. I've done little more than sleep for the last day and a half."

"It takes a lot of energy to heal. And the meds make you tired too. Let's go ahead and get ready for bed. It's been a long day for both of us. And I'll admit you're not the only one who wants more, but I'm going to opt to do what's better for you. It will be worth it in the long run."

"I'm not sure if you're right about that." She didn't want to think about him possibly being right. Her body ached after that kiss, she wanted to see how well he could satisfy that ache. That throb of need that seemed to echo through her entire body. "But I'll take what I can get." She pushed herself upright, struggling for a moment with the heavy brace, but managed to swing her leg off the edge of the bed. "Go get changed. I'll get ready in here." Sitting there, gathering the will to get up, she yawned, then pushed herself to her foot and reached for her crutches.

"Will you be able to manage on your own? Do you need help?" he asked from where he still sat on the bed.

"If I can't manage to get out of these clothes and into my pajamas, I should still be in the hospital," she said, making her way to the table where the bags of her things still sat.

"Also, you don't need to leave things there. There are drawers you can use." He motioned to a chest of drawers against one wall.

"Won't whoever's room this usually is, have things in there? I don't want to run them out."

"Sweetheart, this room was unoccupied before we gave it to you. The drawers are empty." He pulled one out to show her.

She frowned. "Why was the room empty?"

"We keep rooms for people, I keep a room here all the time as do some of the others. Some used to keep rooms but don't anymore." He lifted one shoulder in a half shrug. "It's just how things are. There's nearly always a room if someone wants one, whether for a night, a week or longer. This time it was you."

"Does Chuy keep a room here?"

"He does, though he's not in it as often as he once was. Still, sometimes we've got things going on and it's easier for him to crash here than going home. Sometimes Jill stays with him, but not always."

Jenny nodded, not sure what to say about that.

"If you'd like after I get back from changing, I can help you put things in the drawers. You're going to be here a little while, at least until Giz gets back, you might as well be comfortable."

His offer was sweet, but she wasn't sure she was ready for him to do something quite that intimate. It would be different once they'd slept together, or at least she thought it would be. But since he'd put the kibosh on that idea, she thought she'd rather put her clothes away herself or maybe have one of the women help, if she needed it. But she'd rather try on her own first.

"I'll think about it. Let's get changed first."

"All right. It's up to you. Did you take the pain med with your dinner?"

She shot him a scowl. "Yes, Dad." Why was he so worried about whether or not she took the pills? She didn't like what they did to her mind, but she had to admit, even that was better than sharp stabs every time she moved and the bright burning pain even when she was still.

"I'm not trying to push you into taking them. I'm making sure you didn't forget. If you don't want to take the meds, just say so. But they told you at the hospital to stay ahead of the pain. It's easier to keep it at a maintainable level than to bring it back down once it spikes. I'll go and change, leave you to yourself for a few minutes. If you need anything, call out or call me. If I don't hear you right away, I'll be back in a few minutes."

She nodded but didn't say anything. She had been irritated with his seeming preoccupation with her medication, but now that he mentioned it, she did recall the nurse saying something about staying ahead of the pain. Now she felt bad for snapping at him and resisting his checking on her. Digging through the bag of clothes she found her nightgown and pulled it out. After a moment of debating about whether or not to change here, she opted to take the nightgown into the bathroom to change. She stared at it a moment, wondering the best way to carry it with her, then wrapped it around the back of her neck, reminding of her of how Chuy sometimes did with a towel in the summer when it was hot and he'd been working outside, and headed into the private bathroom.

It took her more than twice as long as she thought it should, but she managed to get changed, as well as brush her teeth, wash her face and brush out her hair, wincing several times as she got too close to the incision from the hole they'd drilled into her head. Her hair had been a chore she probably should have saved for another day but one look at the tangled mess and she couldn't believe Snake had seen past it to be attracted at all, much less kiss her. And he'd been running his hand along it all evening. A shudder passed through her at the thought.

"There you are. I was starting to worry," Snake said from the chair next to the table where he usually sat to wait for her.

"I had to brush out my hair. Why didn't you say anything?" She sat on the foot of the bed and took a deep breath.

"It wasn't important. We would have gotten to it," he said with a shrug. "I would have helped you with it if I knew it was bothering you. Do you want help pulling it up or back?"

"What I'd love is to pull it into a braid, but I don't have the energy for that right now."

"Do you have the energy to sit and let someone else do it for you?"

"Are you going to?"

"I can if you want."

She stared at him for a moment, not sure if she should believe him. "You can braid?"

"I can't do anything fancy like a French braid, but I can pull it back and braid it for you if you like."

"I would like and trust me, by morning, you'll be glad you did." She stood and started for the bathroom.

"Stay where you are. I'll get it. Tell me what you need?"

"The brush and a hair tie, they're both in the blue overnight bag on the edge of the counter." Jenny couldn't help the relief that let her sag back onto the bed. Moving around was so much harder than normal, even the seemingly simple chore of changing clothes had left her exhausted.

He came back with what he needed then told her to sit where she was while he moved onto the bed behind her. It felt so good to have someone else brushing through her hair and messing with it, reminding her of when she was small, and Mom would brush it out after a shower. It had been so long since someone had cared enough to do those little things for her.

She zoned out while he worked with her hair, letting her mind drift with the slight tug and pull of someone styling her hair for her.

"There," he said after a while. "How does that feel?"

"It feels amazing."

"Do you want to see how it looks. I can probably find a mirror for you."

"Doesn't matter how it looks. I'm just going to sleep on it. Thank you." Warmth filled her again that even though she hadn't slept with him – yet – he didn't mind spending time doing things like this with her.

"It's just a braid."

She leaned back until the top of her head touched his chest and she looked up at his face.

"It's a lot more than a simple braid, but I'm too tired to go into it now. Maybe tomorrow. Are you ready for bed?"

"I'm ready whenever you are, sweetheart." He dropped a quick kiss onto her forehead, then waited until she picked her head up before moving. "Let me just put this away. Climb in and I'll join you in a moment." He opened the bathroom door and disappeared inside.

Jenny shoved herself upright once more and maneuvered herself around the side of the bed.

"Do you have a side you prefer?" she called to him.

"Sweetheart, as long as I'm beside you, I'll be happy. Pick the side where you'll be most comfortable."

She thought about it a moment then stacked her crutches and slid into the bed, sliding all the way over so she would lay on the side of her injured leg, so it would be supported and not dangle in the night, making it hurt more.

Snake stepped out of the bathroom as she climbed into the bed, he turned out the lights, then moved to where she'd just gotten in.

"You want me on this side or that one?"

Jenny paused as she thought about it for a moment. Did she want to face him or have him behind her back? Lying against him earlier had felt so nice she scooted backwards and patted the bed in front of her.

"Here."

Once they'd settled into bed, she couldn't resist the urge to slide her hands up his chest, enjoying the sensation of his skin beneath hers, but it didn't last long. He captured her hands and trapped them against his chest with one of his own.

"Sleep, sweetheart, the rest will come soon enough."

"You promise?"

"I promise."

She closed her eyes and drifted off, content that she was safe and cared for.

25

S nake lay for a long time, listening to the soft even sounds of Jenny breathing and trying to make his body behave. Just the feel of her soft and warm against him made his body react as if he were a fifteen-year-old untried boy.

He reminded his body, not for the first time, that no matter how badly they both might want there to be more, her body wasn't ready for it. It would hurt her more than he could make her feel good. Better to wait until they could both enjoy it before they took things farther. It took him a long time to fall asleep.

When Snake woke the next morning, he found himself curled against Jenny's back, one arm wrapped tight around her middle. He wasn't sure if it was to keep her close or what, but he liked the feeling of her pressed against him. It only took him a moment to realize that sometime in the night, her long nightgown had bunched up around her hips and only two thin layers of cotton separating his cock from the round globes of her ass. He lay still, hoping he could talk his body out of reacting, so she could sleep a little longer. He wanted today to be better than yesterday for her, but didn't know how to make that happen.

After what felt like an eon of fighting his body, and failing, she stirred against him, that delectable ass of hers sliding back to press against the erection he was battling, and failing, to control.

He clenched his teeth and closed his eyes again, trying not to react to the way she moved in his arms, making him wish he didn't have half the scruples he did, and had taken her up on her offer last night.

No, even that wouldn't lessen how much he wanted her now.

"Hmm, how long have you been awake?" she said as she opened her eyes and looked up at him.

"Not long."

She wiggled down under the covers with a sigh. The movement rubbed against his wayward cock, and he lost the battle he'd been waging for control. A slow smile curved her lips, making him want nothing more than to taste her again.

"Feels like someone wants some attention." She squirmed again, rubbing her sweet ass against his cock.

Snake clenched his teeth and bit back a groan. "I'll survive. What my body wants isn't what important here. It's what you need."

She wiggled more, and it took him a moment to realize she was trying to roll to face him, but his arm around her middle combined with the weight of her brace was making it more difficult. Snake loosened his hold and waited while she maneuvered, wondering what she had in mind.

When she finally made it into place, she lay snuggled up against his side with one hand resting on his chest. She looked up at him with her hair puffy where strands had come loose from the braid he'd done the night before and lines from the pillow still creasing her face and for some reason he didn't understand, he found her even more attractive than he had when she'd been all decked out, her makeup perfect, at her brother's wedding. Maybe it was that she looked more human, more approachable, he didn't know. All he was sure of was that if he had to wait much longer to get another taste of her sweet mouth, then he wasn't sure what would happen, but it wouldn't be pleasant.

That in mind, he lifted his head and covered her lips with his. Unbelievably, this kiss was even hotter than the one the night before. Snake felt flames lick through his entire body as their tongues tangled. She met him touch for touch and before he knew what was happening, her hand had dipped inside his shorts and wrapped around his cock with a firm grip that nearly had him coming then and there.

That realization brought him back to an awareness he hadn't intended to lose. That awareness told him his hand had slid up under the hem of her nightgown and now his palm was filled with the promising mound of her tit, the nipple firm and pressing into his hand letting him know she was as eager and needy as he was.

"We shouldn't," he said, breaking away from the kiss. "It will hurt you." He couldn't help but notice how his voice had deepened with desire. Damn, the things this woman did to him.

"I can do something that won't hurt." The hand still wrapped around his cock squeezed. She wiggled down in the bed, her gaze still meeting his and the look on her face enough to know she had something in mind. Part of him wanted to let her. The part that burned to find out what she had in mind and if her mouth felt as amazing on his dick as he was sure it would. Another part of him told him no. She wasn't going to get him off if he couldn't return the favor. And he didn't want to come in her mouth, he wanted to feel what he was certain was a hot, sweet pussy squeezing him tight when he erupted inside her. A third part of his brain told him to let her. He could return the favor and if he was careful, he could make her come and watch the pleasure on her face while he did it.

The first part of his brain backed up the third, telling him that eating her pussy wouldn't hurt her, unless he got rough and careless. Besides, from the look on her face, this was something she clearly wanted to do for him. Why should he be the hard case and deny both of them what they both clearly needed?

The heat of her tongue sliding along the length of his cock brought him out of his internal debate and settled the issue then and there. Now that he'd had a sample, there was no way he could stop her. She'd shoved his underwear down and when he saw the look of concentration on her face, his brain short circuited. He could no longer think of a valid reason to stop her.

"Sweetheart—" the words trailed off as she covered the top of his dick with her mouth and slowly pushed it down until her lips surrounded the base. A groan ripped from his throat as she swallowed, and her throat closed around the tip. White hot searing pleasure engulfed his brain. His fingers burrowed into her hair, careful to keep clear of the bandage behind one ear, and he fought the urge to push her down farther or to lift his hips and thrust just a little deeper.

Jenny's gaze flicked up to meet his and he couldn't miss the triumph and pleasure glowing there. She slid her mouth up his length, swirled her tongue around the tip then sank back down again.

Snake groaned. The heat of her mouth and the way she played her tongue over him was more than he'd imagined, and it took everything in him not to lose control.

Instead, he managed to hold on, at least until she used her hands to cup and toy with his balls.

"I'm going to come," he groaned through gritted teeth as he held off as long as he could, wanting to give her a chance to move so he didn't come in her mouth if she didn't want that.

To his surprise, instead of moving, she pushed him deeper in her mouth, sealing her lips around the base of his cock and letting her throat work around the tip of him. That tore away the last of his control and flames raced up his spine as he erupted with a shout.

It wasn't until after he'd finished, and reality and reason finally began to return that he realized he'd curled his hand in Jenny's hair and held her tight as he'd come down her throat.

"I'm sorry, sweetheart. I didn't mean to do that," he said, trying to gently untangle his fingers from her hair.

"Do what?"

"Hold you in place, keep you from moving off me if you didn't want me to come in your mouth. Are you okay? Did I hurt you?"

"I'm fine. I wasn't even aware you'd done it. I wanted you right where you were." Her lips curved upwards.

Snake tugged her up his body until he could reach her to plant another searing kiss on her.

"Can I get rid of this?" he said, breaking the kiss as he lifted the edge of her nightgown.

She lifted one brow and watched him for a split second before pulling the gown off over her head and tossing it aside as if she wasn't going to give him a chance to change his mind.

He rolled her onto her back and gave her a stern look.

"Stay there and tell me if anything I do hurts you." He watched her for a second, then continued, "I'm serious. If you move or I think you're hurting, I'll stop. Understand?" Snake waited until she nodded her agreement before turning his attention to her body.

He let one hand slide down her body, noticing how soft her skin was compared to his, then kissed her again, careful to keep his weight off her. Then he began to trail kisses down her body, pausing at the bend of her shoulder to nip lightly, then sooth the sting away with gentle licks and kisses before continuing on his way.

26

Jenny's breath caught in her throat when Snake's lips closed over her nipple, bolts of sensation shot through her body, sending more heat to pool between her legs. She'd always enjoyed giving blow jobs, they made her feel powerful and in charge, but the way Snake had reacted and how fast he'd gotten off had added something more to the high. She hadn't done it so he would do the same to her, but if he'd decided he could give her a little oral action, who was she to complain or talk him out of it? At least it would give the ache that had been growing low in her belly a bit of relief.

Unable to help herself, she let her eyes close, and her head fall back as all her attention focused on the sensations of what Snake was doing to her body.

He teased her nipples, letting his hands play along her body, touching, squeezing, teasing until every sensation threatened to overwhelm her senses. By the time he trailed kisses down her belly and lower, she was ready to scream with frustration and need.

The heat of his breath across her skin sent goosebumps through her, and when he dropped a soft kiss on top of her mound, Jenny nearly begged him for more. Then his mouth covered her, first giving her a gentle lick, then teasing the sensitive bundle of nerves with more intensity and she didn't have to beg.

Her fingers found their way into his hair, and Jenny soon lost track of what she was doing, time, and the world around them, as all that existed was what Snake made her feel. It didn't take long until her world seemed to explode and when she came back to her senses, he had once more curled behind her, holding her so she felt safe and more content than she could remember feeling, ever.

"Hmmm." She couldn't help the sound of contentment that escaped her, nor did she try.

"Are you okay? I didn't hurt you, did I?" Snake sounded anxious.

"Not at all. I feel amazing." She wasn't about to tell him about the dull throb in her lower leg. He might not touch her again until it was fully healed, and she definitely wanted him to touch her again.

Snake grunted, and she wasn't sure if the sound meant he believed her or not. Either way, he didn't say anything more as she laid her head back, letting it rest in the crook of his arm and let the amazing sense of belonging lull her to sleep.

When she woke later that morning it took Jenny a moment to remember where she was. Between the warm body she found wrapped protectively around her and the unfamiliar surroundings, she couldn't help but feel a little disoriented. She woke slowly, as if pulling her brain out of a vat of tar and trying to make it work again. She blinked several times and tried to force things to function. After a moment, the first time they'd woken that morning before came back to her, in vivid detail.

She remembered asking Snake to stay, and everything that happened after that. A slow smile spread across her face as she remembered how wonderful, how cherished he had made her feel.

"I take it that smile means you're not hurting too bad?" Snake's voice was rough with sleep, sending sparks of heat low in her belly despite the sluggishness of her brain.

She opened her eyes and found him watching her from only a few inches away. It took her a moment to evaluate how she felt. Did she hurt? Yeah, there was an ache in her injured leg that hadn't let up since the accident, but it wasn't any worse than it had been the night before, perhaps even a little better.

"No, not too bad. I feel pretty good. I think a good night's sleep did wonders." She stretched her neck upwards and placed a quick kiss on his cheek. "Thanks for staying with me last night, and even more for this morning."

He twisted a brow as he watched her but remained silent. She couldn't help but wonder what he was thinking but thought perhaps it wasn't the best idea to ask. She might learn something she didn't want to know, at least not yet.

"I guess we should get up?" she said after a moment.

"I need to, but unless you want to, there's no need for you to have to. You need to rest. If you're still sleepy, go back to sleep. The more you rest, the faster you will heal."

She watched him for a moment, trying to decide if the unspoken finish to that might be the faster you'll be out of my hair, was something he meant or if it was just in her head, an echo of her own insecurities. He seemed happy to lay there with her, but who knew what thoughts his face hid?

Jenny took a deep breath and forced herself to get up. I took more strength than she remembered to swing the brace on her injured leg over the edge of the bed and sit up. It wasn't until the blanket and sheet fell away that she recalled she wasn't wearing any clothes. A quick glance around didn't reveal her nightgown, but then, he'd already seen and handled it all, so what was she so worried about?

Jenny stood, careful not to put any weight on her injured leg and glanced around, trying to remember where she'd left her crutches.

"Here." Snake's voice made her twist around to look at him.

She found he had her crutches in hand and was setting them beside her on the edge of the bed. She must have left them on the other side before going to bed.

"Thanks." She wedged them under her arms and made her way first to the chair where the bag with her clothes sat, then into the bathroom to get dressed, refusing to let her mind fixate on the fact that she could feel his gaze on her naked ass as she hobbled away.

27

When Jenny closed the door behind herself, Snake flung back the blanket and stood. He took a moment to straighten up the bed, so Jenny wouldn't have to struggle to get it done, then he pulled on his jeans and went to the door that led out into the hall. He paused with his hand on the knob and turned back.

"I'm going to go get dressed, but I'll be back in a couple minutes. We can go down to breakfast if you'd like," he said, hoping she would hear him.

"Sounds good. I'll see you in a couple minutes." Her voice was slightly muffled, but he had no trouble making out what she said.

That done, he opened the door and stepped out into the hall, then made his way down to his room. He had his hand on the knob to his room when Crash came around the corner and spotted him.

His brother lifted one brow as he took in Snake's state of dress, or half-dressed was maybe more appropriate.

"Busy night? I take it in someone else's room?" He gave the room that had been Snake's since he'd returned from Texas a pointed look. "Since I don't think you're into men, and I know you're not going to go after a brother's woman, I assume you've been with the only single girl in residence. Are you out of your mind? That's Giz's sister. If he finds out you seduced her, he's going to want to wipe up the floor with you."

Snake bit back the urge to get defensive and tell Crash to mind his own fucking business. Instead, he took a deep breath and forced himself to slow down.

"I know who she is. And no, I'm not out of my mind. She asked me to stay with her last night." He wasn't going to go into detail about what had happened between them. No one but he and Jenny needed to know that.

"And your clothes jumped off on their own?" Disbelief was clear in Crash's voice.

"I'm not talking about this with you. It's none of your business, and if you go running to Gizmo with what you've seen, I may need to wipe up the floor with you. When he comes back, I'll deal with me and him, until then, Jenny doesn't want him to know how badly she's been hurt. And until he comes back, I'm making sure she's taken care of."

"Well, that's one way to take care of her that he won't be taking over." Crash's disapproval was clear on his face and in his voice.

Snake ignored him and turned back toward the door. "I need to get dressed. Jenny will be waiting for me to go down and get food. Any other warnings you want to give me?" Snake watched the other Soul with narrowed eyes.

"Your funeral, man." Crash shook his head and continued toward the stairs, leaving Snake to do what he would.

Snake pushed the encounter out of his mind and went into his room to get changed. Jenny was waiting for him.

♦♦♦♦♦♦ ♦♦♦♦♦♦

I t took a little longer to get changed and get back to Jenny than he'd planned but when he knocked on her door, she answered right away, calling out.

"Come in."

He pushed the door open and found her sitting on the edge of the bed, trying to put a shoe on her good foot.

"You ready?"

"I will be in just a minute. I've got to get this shoe on."

"Here, let me help." He moved in and went to his knees and patted one leg. "Set your foot here." He waited until she set her foot on his thigh then gripped the heel and toe. "Is it on good?"

"It's on, but the tongue needs to be pulled out and tied. But I usually prop it on my knee to tie it. But that hurts too much."

"We'll figure it out. We might need to pick you up some slip-on shoes until you get out of that brace, just so you can be independent." He tugged out the tongue and tied her shoe for her, then patted the top of her foot. "In the meantime, I've got no problem helping you." She slid her foot off his leg and used it to stand.

"Thank you, let's go downstairs. I'm hungry." She reached for the crutches and headed for the door.

"Give me your keys." He took them from her and locked the door as she made her way to the stairs then caught up with her in time to hold her crutches while she used the railings to work her way down the stairs. He would rather have carried her, but he was glad she was feeling up to doing it on her own too.

When she reached the ground, he handed her the crutches then followed her to a table and joined her, moving a second chair around for her to rest her leg on so it would hurt less if she ended up sitting here for more than long enough to eat.

They hadn't been there long when Sackett approached and asked what he could get for them.

"That depends on what you have for breakfast," Snake said. "And what you can make without ruining it."

"We have a lot of things, but if you want eggs, I suggest scrambled or over hard. I have a hard time with anything with runny yolks. I can also make pancakes. And I think there are some blueberry muffins in there someone brought in this morning."

Jenny watched Sackett for a moment, as if trying to make up her mind.

"You probably don't have biscuits and gravy ready, do you?"

"Sorry, not today but I can make sure we'll have some tomorrow if you'd like."

"That's not necessary," she said with a smile. "I'll have two pancakes, and do you have any sausage or bacon?"

"We've got both."

"Is the sausage patties or links?"

"I want to say both, but I know we have links. I saw them this morning."

"Then two pancakes, sausage and two scrambled eggs if you don't mind." She smiled at the kid, then looked to Snake, silently telling him it was his turn to order.

"I'll have the same thing but make mine three of each. And coffee."

"Black right?" Savage asked.

"Yes."

"I'll have a cup of coffee too, if you don't mind," Jenny added.

"Not at all. I'll bring you the coffees, then get started on this." He turned and headed for the bar.

Snake turned back to Jenny. "What are your plans for today?"

"I don't know. I don't have any plans really. I thought after we eat, I could go up and put away all my things. Then I'll probably catch up on my email and bills, call my boss and find out what I need to do about work and my disability insurance. I'm sure I'll need something to get that started." She took a deep breath and let it out slowly. "What about you? What are you going to do?"

"I'll help you up to your room then go to work." He watched her for any reaction, was she relieved? Glad to be rid of him for a few hours? She was used to living on her own, having her own space. Living in one room in the middle of the clubhouse for a bunch of men she'd only recently met couldn't be easy for her. The last thing he wanted was to make things more difficult.

"So, you'll be gone until the end of the day." Jenny looked like her mind was spinning a million miles a minute. "I'll probably take a nap after I finish with work. Then I can come back down for dinner."

"Remember. I work next door. I usually come over here for lunch. I would like to have lunch with you too. You can come down here and I'll help you back up or I can bring food up to your room. Whichever you like."

"I'd forgotten you work that close." Some of the tension in her shoulders seemed to disappear. "I would like lunch, but I don't know how I want to do it yet. Can I let you know as it gets closer?"

"Of course. You've got my number right?"

"I do."

"Then if you decide you'd rather have me bring food up to you, just text me what you want, and I'll be happy to do that. Whatever you're more comfortable with."

"Thank you." She seemed to want to say more but Sackett appeared, set cups in front of each of them, then a small dish with cream and sugar packets next to Jenny and poured coffee into both cups.

"Do you need anything else for your coffee?" Sackett asked, looking back and forth between the two of them.

"No, thank you," Jenny said.

Snake shook his head.

"Then I'll go make your breakfast. If you need anything, holler. I'll hear you."

"I'm going to miss him in the kitchen," Snake said once he left.

"Why? Is he going somewhere?" Jenny asked.

"No but we voted to patch him in last night." One corner of his mouth lifted. "I don't think Sadist has even told him yet. But tending bar and working the kitchen is a job we give prospects. They're still figuring out where Boomer will go, and we may keep Sackett around for a while, at least until we see what the other new guy, the one coming in later this week is like, either way we'll have someone here, but Sackett's one of the better cooks we've had."

"Maybe this new guy can cook too."

"If not, he'll learn. We all do, one way or another."

"Even you?"

"Are you asking if I tended bar here or if I can cook?"

"Both."

He couldn't help the smile that quirked his lips as he watched the impish grin she gave him. "That's yes to both, but I could cook before I got here. My first job was in the greasy spoon where my mom waited tables. I started bussing tables when I was barely tall enough to reach across them. I kind of grew up in that place, did my homework at one of the back booths while she worked. As I got older, I did different things. The cook had been teaching me how to make things off and on when there was time, then he got sick and had to be out for several weeks. They were in a panic about replacing him. The owner thought they would have to close until Jack was well enough to come back, but I offered to cook until he came back. They didn't think I could at first, but I proved them wrong. And when Jack got better, we split his shifts at first as he rebuilt his strength."

"That's so sweet."

"It wasn't out of kindness. I got paid to do it, and it was a job I didn't have to hunt for. But it was a good skill and I cooked there until I graduated and left for the Navy."

"From the tattoo I saw, I thought you were in the Navy, but I didn't want to ask. Chuy hates to talk about his time in the military, so I've learned not to ask." Her smile had turned sad and poignant.

Snake covered her hand where it sat on the table with one of his. "Feel free to ask whatever you like. I may not be able to answer and there's a few things I won't want to for one reason or another. I won't lie to you either way. I'll tell you straight out I don't want to or can't tell you. But I want you to feel like you can talk to me about anything."

"I'll try to remember that. But I'll admit, when I thought to ask you about it, it wasn't the right time and you'd pushed all thoughts about it out of my head by the time it was a good time."

She met his gaze and pulled her lower lip between her teeth. Her face flushed. He knew she had to be remembering the tattoo on his chest. Snake hadn't thought much about it in the last few years, but once it had been the most important thing in his life. The symbol of his unit and the men he'd been as close to as the Souls were now.

It wasn't that he'd forgotten them, but those of them that were left had drifted into their own lives. He heard from a couple now and then, but not often. Still, they were his brothers, and he could reach out to them if he needed to.

28

By the time Jenny finished finding homes for all the things Krissi, Beth and Elyse had brought her from home, then called her boss about her disability insurance, she was surprised by how exhausted she was. She didn't think she'd done all that much. She certainly hadn't expended as much energy as she usually did in a shift at work, but it was all she could do to hold her head up or keep her eyes open.

She had hoped to wait until after lunch to take a nap, but she didn't think she was going to make it. Exhausted, she sat in one of the chairs next to the table and reached for her phone, but found her pocket empty.

Crap.

What had she done with it?

Looking around for it, Jenny spotted it on the table next to the bed, plugged in. She propped her head in her hand, elbow resting on the table next to her and stared at the phone, trying to will it to fly across the room and land in her hand. Failing that, she would wait a few minutes until she could muster the energy to get up again and go get it so she could let Snake know she was going to skip lunch and nap instead.

Jenny was jarred awake as a knock sounded on her bedroom door, making her jump and her head fall from where it had been resting in her hand. She blinked, trying to remember where she was and why she was sleeping sitting up, but the knock sounded again.

"Come in," she called, just to get the noise to stop.

"Hey, sweetheart, you didn't tell me what you wan—" Snake's words cut off as he spotted her. "Hey, are you all right?"

"Yeah. Fine." She blinked again, trying to clear the fog from her mind. "I must have fallen asleep. I was going to text you and let you know I was too tired for lunch. I'm sorry. I didn't mean for you to come up and waste your lunch time."

"Don't worry about it, sweetheart. Mac is flexible, but more important than that is you." He stepped into the room and crouched so he was eye to eye with her. "Are you sure you're all right?"

"I'm fine. Just tired. I finished cleaning up and putting away my things and realized I could barely keep my eyes open. I was going to send you a message about lunch then lay down and take a nap, but it seems like I fell asleep before I made it to my phone." She motioned to the bedside table where her phone still sat.

"That's okay. You needed the rest, obviously. The question now is now that you've had a little sleep, do you want to lay back down, or do you want lunch?"

"I still don't feel like eating. I do feel like I can make it to the bed though, so there's that. But I feel bad about you coming all the way up here."

"No bother. I've got all the time I need and I'm glad I got to see you. Want help making it to bed?"

She looked up at him through her lashes, considering it.

"I can manage, thanks." She leaned close and kissed his cheek. "Thanks for taking care of me. I'm starting to see why you didn't want me home alone. And with food and help here around the clock, I see why you set me up here. I just miss my bed and my own place."

"We'll get you back there soon. Come on. Let me help you get to bed, then I'll go eat while you rest. I'm sure by dinner time you'll feel better."

She looked at the bed and the expanse of floor between her and it, then at him. "I can do it but thank you for the help. For some reason, I'm just exhausted. I didn't do that much. I shouldn't be this tired." She picked up her crutches and used them to help leverage herself to her feet. "I don't want to lay on top, can you pull the blankets back? I can make it over there on my own."

"No problem." He moved ahead of her and laid the blankets back before stepping out of her way and watching as she made her way over and sat on the edge of the bed. She knew he was ready to help if she needed it, but she didn't. As soon as she sat, he took the crutches and leaned them against the bedside table. "Is there anything else I can get you?"

Jenny shook her head as she tried to kick off the shoe he'd helped her with his morning. He saw her struggling and peeled the shoe off without a word.

"Thanks," she said, swinging her feet up onto the mattress once it was off. Lying down felt heavenly. Better than she could remember, and she'd only been out of bed for a few hours.

Once he made sure she didn't need anything, he left, closing the door as he went. Jenny wondered how long she would feel like such a slug because she didn't have the strength to do what she wanted.

29

M ore disappointed than he wanted to admit, or even look too closely at, Snake made his way back down to the main floor of the clubhouse and ordered his lunch from Savage. It wasn't that he was upset about it. In fact, he was happy she was resting. What had him frowning as he stared at nothing was that she'd fallen asleep at the table without intending to.

It made him worry that she was pushing herself too hard and doing too much. While she might think she was just trying to get things done, he knew from experience that it could set back her recovery. The idea of her taking longer to heal gave him mixed feelings. He wanted her to feel better. If she felt better, she'd be happier and something deep inside him wanted to see her happy. The mixed part was harder to look at, even for him. If her healing took longer, it was longer she could rely on him. While the idea appealed to him, he didn't want to look too closely at why. Instinct told him looking too closely at that side of the double-edged sword might reveal something about himself he wasn't ready for.

But he knew he wasn't ready for her to walk away from him. Just the idea of it sent his stomach into a flutter of panic.

"Here you are. I saw you come down. Did Jenny want anything?" Savage asked as he set the plate in front of Snake.

Snake shook his head. "She's going to take a nap. She may call down for something, or she may not. I'll check on her again when I get off for the day. If she doesn't ask for something between now and then, I'm sure she'll be down for dinner."

"No problem. Anything else I can get you?" Savage looked down at the plate, then back to Snake, brows lifted.

Snake looked around the table, checking for his drink and flatware. "I don't think so. Thanks."

The prospect went back to what he was doing, something behind the bar that Snake hadn't paid any attention to. Snake turned his attention to this meal, determined to get through lunch and the rest of the work shift without thinking about Jenny.

He hadn't even finished his lunch before he failed.

❦

S nake replaced the drain plug in the oil pan of the car that had come in twenty minutes ago for an oil change. It was a job that he could have done in his sleep, and probably had sometime in the not too distant past, but Snake didn't mind. Yes, there were more interesting, more engaging jobs in the shop today, but since he found his mind kept drifting back to Jenny and wondering how she was doing, so the simple, repetitive jobs were perfect for him, at least today.

Gizmo was also present in his thoughts and how he would tell his friend what had happened while he was gone, not just the truth about Jenny's accident, but what was developing between himself and Jenny. Snake wouldn't tell him the details, obviously, but he wasn't going to hide that he was with Jenny, for however long it lasted.

By the time he finished with the oil change it was quitting time. He washed up and headed over to the clubhouse. He hoped Jenny was awake and feeling better.

"Snake, I need to see you," Sadist's voice called across the clubhouse as he stepped inside and waited for his eyes to adjust to the dimmer interior.

"Can it wait ten minutes?" Snake asked. "I'm on my way to check on Jenny."

"No rush. It's important but not urgent. Any time tonight will be fine," the VP said with a wave of one hand.

Snake wondered what was up as he mounted the stairs, taking them two at a time in his hurry to see if she was awake and how she felt.

Outside her door, he listened for a moment, trying to pick up any sounds of movement, but heard nothing. Was she still sleeping?

He knocked, rapping gently on the door, not wanting to wake her if she was sleeping, and not certain if he hoped she was awake or asleep as she obviously needed it if she was sleeping, but she also needed to eat in order to fuel healing.

Snake was saved from having to worry about it when she called out, bidding him inside. He opened the door and stepped inside to find her sitting up in bed, almost in the same spot where he'd left her hours before.

"How are you feeling this evening?" Snake said in greeting.

"Better, I think. At least I'm awake." She blinked several times.

"Are you hungry?"

She stared at him for a moment, as if her brain wasn't working quite as quickly as she was used to.

"Yeah, but it's going to be a bit before I'm ready. I want to take a shower first."

"All right. Do you need help, or do you want me to leave you to it and call me when you're ready to come down?"

Her cheeks turned pink. "Would you mind waiting a few minutes to make sure I can get in on my own? Then you can go do whatever you need to while I finish up? I want to see if I can shower on my own. I'll call when I'm ready to go downstairs."

"Not at all. I need to go talk to Sadist anyway. Take your time and let me know when you're ready. Just be careful of that incision behind your ear. I'll let you know if I need to leave for any reason, and who will be here to help, if you need it, okay?"

"Sure."

She'd started moving, and gathered a couple of things, taking them into the bathroom with her. He sat at the table and listened in case she called out for help. After several minutes she called out, her voice a little muffled because of the door but still understandable.

"I'm good. You can go do you're thing now. I'll call if I need anything."

He shot one last look at the bathroom door before letting himself out of her room. Snake stood in the hallway outside her door for a moment as he debated heading to his room and cleaning up a little, but dismissed the idea and decided to go see what Sadist needed.

"What's up, boss?" he asked as he approached the table where the VP sat.

"Couple of things. First, I want to know how Gizmo's sister is doing."

"She's okay. She isn't thrilled with being here instead of at home, but she now understands why we insisted she come here. She's healing. Not as fast as she would like, I'm sure. But she is healing. She slept most of the afternoon, which is good for her, it will help her heal. When I checked on her, she said she wanted to shower, and she'd let me know when she's ready to come down." He patted the pocket where his phone rested. That reminded him. He needed to make sure it wasn't silent. He pulled out his phone, checked it and put it back, while he waited for the VP to ask his next question.

When he looked back at the VP, he met the man's gaze.

"Are you sure sleeping with her is the best way to take care of your brother's sister?" Sadist didn't pull any punches or bother to dance around the issue that was on his mind.

"Damn Crash." Snake shook his head. "I won't say I didn't have second thoughts about it, but it wasn't what it looked like. She asked me to stay. I didn't seduce her."

"And do you think that will help her heal?"

"Fuck." He should have known that nothing would stay private in the clubhouse. "Nothing happened to hurt her leg. I won't kiss and tell, but I want her better as much as anyone else." He didn't say that he wanted it probably more, partly because he wasn't willing to look at why he wanted it. Whether it was so she could move on with her life or so he could see her more, wasn't something Sadist needed to know. Fuck it wasn't even something Snake could answer right now.

Sadist watched him a moment longer. Snake wasn't sure how to read the look but kept a straight face, he might not be doing what was right, but he wasn't wrong either. The way he saw it, he was in kind of a gray area, and wasn't that where most of the Souls lived their whole lives?

"How would you feel if Jenny were your sister and another of the Souls slept with her? Can you put yourself in that position?" Sadist twisted a brow as he waited for an answer.

Snake's gut churned. "I wouldn't like it. I know what we are here, she doesn't. But I have been careful not to make a move on her. She has made every first move and I'm trying to behave myself and be the best brother I can be. That said, we all know I'm not a saint. Hell. None of us are. Sure as hell not Gizmo. Especially before he met Jill." Snake had been gone for two years, but he hadn't forgotten what their tech sergeant was like back then. He'd been a bit of a slut, taking on any challenge and nearly any woman.

"I know that. And I'm not saying you're in the wrong here. Just a warning to know what you're doing. And not to shit where you eat." Sadist met his gaze, as if making sure Snake understood his meaning.

He did and he had no intention of making a mess, but wasn't that usually how things started?

Fuck. Snake was so out of practice with relationships he couldn't be sure he wasn't screwing things up royally. Not that it was any of Sadist's business, but maybe he should tell Jenny. Either way he was through discussing it with his VP.

"Is that all?"

"No, actually, it's not." Sadist looked around the room, making sure there was no one near to overhear. "We've had some trouble with a shipment, and I need you to go check it out." He held up a hand to forestall the argument Snake had on the tip of his tongue. "I know you are busy with Jenny and don't want to venture far from her, but I need you on this. I'll make sure Jenny's cared for, but I need someone I know can handle whatever the issue is. Right now, that's you."

Snake clenched his teeth and bit back the urge to argue. It would do him no good and only delay what was inevitable anyway.

"All right, where are they?"

Sadist gave him a few details, mostly the location of where to meet the group and a broad rundown of what was going on. Snake didn't know if the briefing was short on details because they were in the main room of the clubhouse or because Sadist didn't know much. He leaned toward the latter as it would only have been a few steps until they could be in the secure back room where they were safe to talk about sensitive subjects and Sadist never suggested they step in there.

"Do you need me out there now or can it wait until after dinner?" He glanced up at the second-floor railing, making sure Jenny hadn't decided to try to make it down the stairs on her own.

"I need you to head out tonight, it's not too far or I would say go in the morning, but it can wait until after you've eaten. And had a chance to tell Gizmo's sister you're going to be away for a bit."

Snake didn't have to see Sadist's scowl to know it was a warning about how much he told her. Not being able to share what was going on in his life was a big part of why it had been so long since he'd had any kind of relationship with a woman. He had hook ups while he'd been in Texas but no one he could talk to, no one he wanted to talk to or spend more time with than it took to get off and move on.

That wasn't what he wanted with Jenny, no matter what his VP might think.

"Ten-four. I'll head out as soon as I get her settled after dinner. Will I need a truck?" What Snake didn't say was that he'd be handling the situation as quickly as he could so he could get back to her.

"It's some problem with one of the bikes. Something that needs fixed but not serious enough to stop them, that's why it's not so urgent, but you'll want to take the truck. Oh, Puck's coming in tonight too. I know I asked you to give him the tour but since you'll be off taking care of this little problem, I'll take care of it."

Sadist turned his attention to the notebook in front of him. Snake didn't know what he was studying so hard and wasn't about to ask. It might get him more of an assignment than the one he had and that was enough for now, plus, now he didn't have to worry about watching out for the new guy.

He went to the bar and asked for a soda from Savage. He wanted a beer, but not if he needed to be on the road tonight. He'd made it about halfway through the drink when his phone buzzed in his pocket. A quick check told him it was Jenny. She was ready to come down for dinner. He took his soda and set it on the table he would bring Jenny down to, then hurried up the stairs.

By the time they'd made it back down to the main floor, Savage had added a drink for Jenny to the table and as soon as they were seated and comfortable, the prospect reappeared.

"What can I get you for dinner tonight?"

"What's your best meal?" Jenny asked, surprising Snake.

"What do you mean?" Savage frowned, clearly not understanding.

"What are you the best at making?"

"I can do a killer burger. I'm not bad at pastas either, but I made a big pan of enchiladas this afternoon. I think that's my best thing."

"What kind? Red or green?"

"Red sauce, but they have green chili in them," Savage said.

"Perfect. That's what I'll have. A bit of sour cream on the side, if you have it, please."

"We do. Want guac too?"

Jenny shook her head.

"I'll take the burger," Snake said. He wasn't one to complain but he'd had little more than Mexican food while he'd been in Texas. It had been good, but he was ready for a change.

The prospect took their drink orders then left them alone.

"What are your plans for this evening?" Snake asked after a couple moments.

"I don't have any. I hadn't even thought about it. But honestly what sounds the best is going back up to my room and maybe watching something, but more likely going back to sleep. It sounds stupid because I've slept most of the day, but it's all I feel like doing tonight." Her face flushed and she looked away as if embarrassed.

"No, it makes perfect sense. You're injured that means your body is using more energy than you're used to, plus everything you do takes more energy than normal because you're hauling this along with you." He laid on hand on the brace covering her lower leg. "And I may be wrong, but I think you may have pushed a little too hard this morning, both before we got up and after breakfast, so that's coming back to bite you in the ass." He kept his voice gentle and hoped she wouldn't be offended by his blunt observation.

She stared across the room as she took a deep breath and let it out slowly. He wasn't sure if she was trying to hold her temper or considering his words.

"As much as I hate admitting it, you may be right. I probably did too much this morning and over tired myself." She sighed. "I'm not used to this and it's taking some adjustment. Do you mind if I go back up and go back to bed?"

"No. Not at all. I was going to let you know I've got something I've got to do, and I don't know how long it's going to take. I'm pretty sure if I get back tonight, it will be late. But I'll make sure there's someone here in case you need anything."

Jenny frowned. "Something you need to do?" She glanced around the room, but her gaze returned to him.

"Yeah. It's club business and I'm not even sure what it is yet. But I'll deal with whatever it is and get back here as quickly as I can. I don't want to leave you for too long."

She shook her head, her scowl growing even deeper.

"Don't worry about it. I'm a big girl and can take care of myself, mostly. And over the last couple days I've learned to ask for help." Her scowl turned to a wry smile. "The results of not asking aren't worth the little bit of embarrassment it costs me to ask."

"Why does it embarrass you to ask for help?" Snake tilted his head and watched her.

She lifted her shoulders and let them drop. "I don't know. It doesn't bother me to ask Chuy for help, but I have a hard time when it's anyone else. Well, except for you. I can ask you now and not feel bad about it. But anyone else? I just have a hard time doing it."

"Then I guess I'll have to hurry back to make sure you don't go without just because you don't want to ask."

"I won't do that." She shook her head and looked away. "I don't want you to hurry and get hurt. Do what you need to do, but get some rest before you come home. You've been up all day and you're leaving again soon. Don't get hurt trying to get back to me, please."

She looked up and met his gaze. The pleading there made something catch in his chest, and an ache spread through him that he couldn't name.

"I'll play it by ear. If I'm too tired to come back when I get done, then I'll get some rest first. Okay?" What he didn't say was he had no idea how long whatever Sadist wanted him to do would take. He might not be finished with this chore until daylight, or possibly later.

"Okay. How was your day? Anything interesting happen while I slept?" She got her question out as Savage arrived with their dinners. Snake waited until the prospect left before answering.

"Nothing that I know of. I worked in the shop all day, other than when I came over for lunch. I got you into bed and ate while I was here, then went back to work. Haven't heard any news or seen anything, other than Sadist asking me to handle whatever this job is tonight."

They ate, exchanging a few words here and there. By the time they finished eating, she was drooping in her seat again. He waited until she was ready before he helped her up to her room and got her settled, then after making sure she had the number of the bar downstairs as well as the women and several of the men hanging around the clubhouse that evening, he knew he couldn't put it off any longer.

As much as he wanted to feel the wind in his face and the rumble of the bike beneath him, he grabbed several things from the shop where he worked, including a large toolbox, and loaded it all into his pickup then climbed inside. If someone had some kind of trouble with their bike that hadn't stopped them but had slowed them. He needed to get it fixed so they could finish the run. Even if that wasn't the trouble, it wouldn't hurt to be prepared.

Snake clenched his teeth as he started the engine and pulled out onto the street. He didn't want to have to do this, whatever it was. He wanted to be curled up in the bed upstairs with Jenny.

But we don't always get what we want, Snake knew that and since his first commitment wasn't to her but to the Souls, he did what he'd been asked to.

It took Snake over three hours to get to the rest of the men who were on the run Sadist had asked his help with. They had barely made it through Phoenix when they'd stopped to wait for him. They hadn't been as far ahead of him as he'd thought, or maybe they'd been taking out of the way roads.

He found the men, all six of them, pulled off I-17 just north of New River.

"Hey, Wally, what's up?" Snake asked, approaching the brother closest to him.

"You need to talk to Mac. He's in charge of this thing," the older man said with a wave of his hand toward Snake's day-to-day boss.

Snake clenched his teeth and resisted the urge to snap at the man who'd been one of the original Demented Souls and instead approached Mac.

"How's it going?" Snake said in greeting.

"Not as well as I'd hoped." Mac slapped Snake on the back in greeting. "I take it you're the one Sadist sent to help us out?"

Snake nodded and looked around, trying to figure out which bike was the one with the problem.

"It's Sackett's bike that's the problem." Mac shook his head. "His front wheel moves too much at higher speeds. We could keep at the lower speeds until now, so it wasn't too noticeable, but for the next hundred or so miles, we're on the interstate, and the slower speeds will make us more noticeable and more likely to get stopped."

Snake nodded, he knew why they didn't want to get stopped, it could lead to a search and that was the last thing they needed while hauling weapons of questionable legality.

"You think it's the head bearing?" Snake watched the older man.

"I do. It was fine when we checked things out before leaving. But he says he hit a rock about a hundred or so miles ago and it started this. We called for help as soon as we noticed it, but Sadist told us to keep moving as long as it wasn't too dangerous. I've been watching him and thinking about it and I'm about ninety percent sure that's the problem. This isn't the ideal place to do a repair like that, but it could be worse. At least this is something we should be able to do, and test, fairly quickly. If I'm right, we can get back on the road and send you home. I just didn't have the right tools with me. I hope you brought them." Mac sent a pointed glance at Snake's pickup.

"If they're in the carry box, I brought them. It has the best assortment of stuff for working on bikes, so it's what I grabbed. I've also got a few parts, but not knowing what was wrong with it, I could only guess. I tried to think of what could be done on the side of the road without too much fuss, and bring what was needed for those repairs."

"Did you think to bring a jack?"

Snake let a smile curve his lips. "This ain't my first rodeo. If you've got to do a repair, it might go a little faster or easier with a jack, so I made sure I had one in the truck." He didn't mention that he kept one there for his bike just like he kept one there for the truck itself. He'd started doing it years before.

The two of them worked together, much as they had so many times in the shop, and before an hour passed, they'd finished the adjustment and put the tools back in the box.

"I want you to take this out for a test drive," Snake said to Sackett. "Don't get up on the interstate, but take a back road, find a deserted spot, and run the speed up as high as you dare. Try to make it do what it was before."

Sackett nodded his understanding, then climbed off the bike and took off.

"How much you willing to bet that fixes it?" Snake glanced over at Mac.

"Cash? Not much, but that's because I don't have much on me. What's your point?"

"Do we take the risk and load up the tools or do we wait for him to get back before putting everything up?"

Mac frowned, then pursed his lips for a couple moments before speaking, "Load them up. If that didn't work, whatever the problem is won't be fixed on the side of the highway. We'll redistribute our load, put his bike in the truck and send him home with you." Mac stared in the direction Sackett had taken. "I thought about just sending him back on his own, but I don't like the idea of him on his own. He's just gotten his colors and who knows how he'd react if someone tries to cause trouble with him."

Snake nodded, it was hard to tell how anyone would deal with a situation until they'd been in some kind of conflict, and while Sackett had been with the Souls longer than Snake had been back, he didn't know him all that well personally. At least not yet. If the repair hadn't fixed the problem with his bike, it looked like he might get the opportunity to know him better.

While they waited for Sackett to return, and while packing the tools into the box and the box into the back of Snake's truck, they chatted about work, the ride so far and plans for the next few days. Thirty minutes after he'd left, Sacket came back, a huge grin spread across his face as he pulled the bike to a stop alongside Snake's truck.

"It's good. I found a long straight stretch and ran it up to one-ten. No wobble, nothing. You did it!" The newest Soul's enthusiasm was contagious, and Snake found himself grinning back.

"I'm glad. This is an emergency fix. It may be all it needs, but after this run, bring it into the shop and let us take a look at it, just to make sure you don't have any more problems."

"Will do!" The kid gave him a mock salute.

Snake rolled his eyes and bit back the urge to tell him to knock it off. He wasn't an officer, and the kid should know better, but he knew the kid was just being a smart ass since Snake had been issuing orders.

They spent a few minutes getting things arranged and men back on bikes and Snake checked his watch as he watched the crew hit the road and get back on their way. He wondered how much farther they would ride tonight, and where they planned to stop.

Should he trail along after them in case there was more trouble? At pushing ten, it was starting to get late. He should have asked Mac what the plan was, but it hadn't occurred to him before they'd pulled out.

Now he was torn between making sure his brothers finished the run with no difficulty and being there for Jenny. He started after them until long after their taillights disappeared among all the others on the interstate then concluded that Mac was a grown man who would have asked him to trail after them if he'd felt they needed it. He wouldn't appreciate Snake deciding he knew more than the veteran biker, and following them.

With some reluctance, but eagerness too, he got back in the truck and headed south, back to Tucson. He wasn't sure he'd make the whole trip tonight. If he drove straight through, he'd get back to the clubhouse at around one a.m. While that wasn't too late for him, he was sure Jenny would be long since asleep. In the end he decided to get back tonight. He'd rather have that drive now, than in the morning when he could spend at least a bit of time with her.

30

The sun streaming in the one high window in her room woke Jenny the next morning. She lay for a moment letting her brain wake up, then she stretched and threw the covers back before she struggled to get up and wished for what felt like the millionth time that she could get rid of the stupid brace.

It was a struggle, but she took care of her needs and managed to get dressed. She'd found out loose pants or skirts worked best with the brace, but shorts or short skirts left her too cold. It was early in the year for things like that. She was combing out her hair and trying to decide what she wanted to do with it when a knock sounded on her door.

"It's open," she called, hoping it would be Snake. Other than Krissi and the other women, he was the only one who ever knocked without her calling first.

"Hey, sweetheart, how did you sleep?" Snake's voice made her smile as she continued to try to work the snarls from her hair.

"Hard." She gave a brief laugh. "I couldn't tell you how long I slept, but I don't think I moved all night. I don't even know if I dreamed. Are you just getting back? How far did you have to go last night?"

"The other side of Phoenix. It wasn't too bad."

"Did you just get back?" She hadn't checked the time, but knew it had to be late for the sun to have hit that window to wake her. Now looked at the clock next to the bed and found it was nearly ten. She was blown away that she'd managed to sleep that late.

"No, I came in last night. I slept late this morning, and I've only been awake an hour or so. I was waiting for you to wake up and call or text, but it got late enough I was starting to worry." Snake stepped up beside her and held out a hand. "Here, let me help you with that."

She only hesitated for a moment before laying the brush in his hand. He started working the brush through her hair, taking his time, being careful of her incision, and working through the snarls with far more patience than she'd used. Jenny closed her eyes and enjoyed having someone else care for her hair.

"Want me to pull it up or braid it?"

"A braid would be good." Warmth spread through her that he cared enough to take care of it for her. Plus, it would be out of her face, and she wouldn't have to worry about what it looked like.

"Give me a second. Do you have a hair tie?"

She picked up one from the bag in front of her and held it up for him. It didn't take him long to finish twisting her hair into a neat braid and after his last effort, she didn't feel the need to double check his work to see how she looked.

"There, all done. Anything else you need to do? Or are you ready to go get something to eat?" Snake asked, handing her the brush back.

Jenny put the brush back into the zipper pouch she used for her hair things.

"I only have one thing left to do and I hate to ask for help with such a simple thing, but I haven't picked up any slip-on shoes yet and it's too cool out for flip flops." She held out her good foot, showing him it was bare.

"Not a problem. Where's your sock?" He moved around in front of her and sat on his heels before lifting her foot to rest in his lap.

She handed him the sock and watched as he slipped it onto her foot before picking up her shoe and doing the same. She couldn't believe her luck that he would help her with such basic needs without complaint or making her feel like she should be able to do it on her own.

Nearly as quickly as she could have done it herself, without the injury that made it difficult, Snake set her foot back on the floor and stood.

"There. Ready to go get something to eat?"

Her stomach chose that moment to rumble loudly. She couldn't help but laugh at the timing.

"I am. And just in time it seems." She stood and reached for her crutches. She handed him the key to her room then headed for the door. Outside the room in the hallway, she didn't wait for him but started for the stairs knowing it would take her longer to get there and down than it would him. When she reached the stairs, he hadn't yet caught up with her, so she stacked her crutches and leaned them against the railing, then started down.

By the time she reached the bottom, he was right behind her, crutches in hand. She took them and tucked them under each arm before looking up at him.

"Where do you want to sit?" she asked.

"Wherever you do."

She shot him a disgruntled frown then headed for the table they usually sat at. As she sat, and while she was still trying to get comfortable, Savage appeared with another guy she didn't think she'd ever seen before trailing behind him. He set two coffee cups in front of them, and a small dish of coffee condiments in front of her before filling both cups. When he'd done that, he moved the chair she rested her leg brace on closer and waited until she was situated.

"This is Puck, he's new around here and following me around to learn a bit before we toss him in the deep end. Are you wanting breakfast food or lunch?" Savage said once she'd settled.

Jenny looked at him, then to the man behind him, she smiled. "Nice to meet you."

He nodded but didn't reply.

She didn't know if he was nervous or if it was something else, either way not her business. She took a deep breath and let it out slowly as she considered her options. "I think I'll go with lunch. What sounds amazing to me right now is a burger and fries."

"No problem. How do you want it?" He pulled a pad from his pocket and took notes as she told him. Then he turned to Snake for his order. When he had down what they both wanted, Savage hurried off.

"I know it was club business and you can't tell me, so I won't ask what you were doing last night. I will ask how it went. Since you came back last night, I assume there was no big trouble?"

He stared at her for a moment, as if trying to decide how much he could say. "No. No big trouble. I met up with some of our men who are out on a run, you know what a run is?"

"Kind of. It's like an organized ride, right?"

"It is, sometimes we have a reason, sometimes it's just for brotherhood. We had some things that needed to go north, and these guys just decided they wanted to go up and see the Grand Canyon while they were up that way. They offered for everyone to go, but I didn't want to leave you."

"You didn't have to do that. I could have gotten by." She felt bad that he'd stayed behind so he could be with her. Jenny also wanted to ask what needed to go north that they could take on their motorcycles, but since he hadn't volunteered what it was, maybe it was something he couldn't tell her about? She knew her brother wouldn't be involved in people who ran drugs not since they were the reason it had been just the two of them for so long. Other than that, she could wait.

"Don't worry about it." Snake waved one hand in dismissal. "I had other things keeping me here, like work. Besides, it's cold up there still. I would rather go see a giant crack in the ground in a couple months once I'm not going to freeze my ass off on the trip." He gave her a lopsided grin. "Maybe by then you'll be up to going with me." He didn't wait for a response but kept talking, "Anyway, one of them was having trouble with his bike but they didn't have the tools with them for the repair." He lifted one shoulder and let it drop. "I took a toolbox and a truck and met them along the way. It took us less than an hour to get his bike fixed and they hit the road again."

"And you drove back."

"And I drove back. I considered finding a room somewhere, but it wasn't that late, and I knew I'd sleep better here. Between being in my own bed and knowing I was near if you needed anything, both made me more comfortable."

With that kind of reasoning, she really couldn't argue. Though she could say she hadn't needed him, she had to admit, at least to herself, that she liked knowing he was thinking about her.

She nodded and decided it was time to change the subject. "What's the plan for today?"

"I thought you might like to get out of here for a while. We might go by your place if you want to get something there or hit a store. Though I will be finding, and you will be using one of those motorized carts." He frowned and pinned her with a look that said she wouldn't be arguing her way out of that one.

She was so happy at the idea of getting out of for a while she wasn't even going to fight the scooter thing. "A little shopping sounds heavenly." She tried to think of what she needed. Shoes she could put on by herself, shampoo and conditioner, what the girls had given her wasn't bad, but she preferred her own brand. There was more, she was sure, but nothing else came to mind off hand. She looked down at what she had on and decided it was as good as she was going to get with what was available. "How soon can we leave? Don't you have work?"

"After we eat, and no. I'm taking today off after that trip last night. There's no rush. I thought we could get what you need at the store, maybe go to a park so you can get a little sunshine. I know it can't be easy being stuck in here all the time."

"Sunshine sounds amazing." She wasn't going to say anything, but being stuck in one building all the time was getting to her. Still, she'd been enough trouble, she wasn't about to ask for something more.

"I don't want to do too much and exhaust you again, so we'll play it by ear and see how you feel."

She was saved from having to respond right away by Savage bringing their food. He served them, asked if they needed anything else then left them to eat. She was hungry enough she didn't wait to dig in.

31

After they finished eating, Snake followed Jenny out to his pickup, helped her into the passenger's seat, then stowed her crutches in the rear seat so she could reach them when they stopped. After going around and getting into the driver's seat, he started the engine then looked at her.

"Where to first?"

"Isn't there a Target a few blocks down this way?" She pointed to the north.

Snake paused, checking his mental map. "Yeah, is that where you want to go?"

"It's as good as any. Plus, a Walmart is farther, much farther if we go for a big one."

"I'm up for whatever you want." He watched her, waiting for a decision before he pulled out onto the road.

"You don't mind going farther to go to Walmart?"

"Not at all. Which one you want to go to?" He watched a series of emotions flash across her face and couldn't help wondering what she was thinking and if he really wanted to know how her mind worked.

"I'd really prefer Walmart, the one up on La Cholla is my favorite."

The idea made him pause. Did he have a favorite store of any kind, well other than a restaurant? He pulled out onto the road and thought about it for a moment as he navigated traffic.

Yeah, he did, they were just different kinds of stores. Sadist Den was his favorite tattoo shop, Drifters was his favorite bar, though he wasn't sure that would count. Now that he'd thought of those, he knew there had to be more.

"What are you thinking so hard about over there?" Jenny's voice pulled him from his ruminations.

"You got me thinking."

"About what?"

"Favorite stores. Until you said that, I would have laughed and dismissed the idea, then I realized I do have favorites. They're just a different kind of store than Walmart."

"What are some of your favorite places?"

He glanced over at her, wondering if she would laugh or be put off by his favorites. It only took a moment, but he decided he'd rather know than not.

"Sadist Den, Drifters, a couple of local diners. I was going to say Mac's but that probably doesn't count."

"It doesn't, but not for the reason you probably think."

"Why doesn't it count?" He glanced at her with a twisted brow, then turned his attention back to the road.

"Because it's where you work. I mean it's good you like being there and all, but it's your job, not somewhere you like to shop."

"But the bar counts?" He shot her a glance before looking back to the road. Traffic wasn't too bad, but it was the heavy time of year, and he didn't know how her accident might have affected her, so he was being careful.

"Bar?" She narrowed her eyes at him. "I think maybe you better tell me what kind of places you're naming. I assume Sadist Den wasn't the bar?"

He shook his head. "It's Sadist's tattoo shop. The bar is Drifters."

"Let me guess. One of the Demented Souls owns it?"

"Yeah, it's Ruger's. Why?"

"It carries. The other two places you've mentioned are owned by your brothers, it just made sense that one was too."

He shot her a look from the corner of his eye, trying to decide if she was messing with him or if she was serious. How should he take it that he was that predictable?

"Is it a problem?"

"Not at all. It makes sense. They're your brothers. You like them, you spend time with them, it makes sense that you'd spend time in their businesses."

Since he'd spent the last two years trying to keep from being predictable or being tied to his brothers by people who might be looking a little too closely at him, to find this out rubbed him wrong. He pushed that away. He wasn't in Texas or undercover anymore. He needed to get past the mindset that had saved his life then and back into the groove of life here in Tucson.

There was no one on his tail, no one looking to kill him and his brothers if they made one slip up. That wasn't to say everything was on the up and up, but they all had some defense here in their home turf. At least he wasn't looking over his shoulder everywhere he went and didn't have to be paranoid about someone watching him every time he got that itch on the back of his neck.

Come to think of it, he didn't think he'd felt that itch since he'd returned. It was something he didn't miss and hoped never to feel again.

"You're thinking too hard again." Jenny's voice made him glance over at her and smile. He liked that she didn't let him brood.

"Just thinking."

"Can I ask about what?"

"You can always ask, but I'm afraid I can't answer," he shot her a sad smile, "or more accurately, I can't answer in a way that makes sense. I'd have to leave too much out."

She frowned but didn't complain. He couldn't help but wonder how long that would last.

In his experience, any time he couldn't tell a woman what he was doing or where he was going, eventually it led to suspicions and distrust. Which eventually led to the end of the relationship. Would Jenny be any different? Would her brother being a Soul make a difference? Were they even in a relationship or was it all in his head? Thoughts swirled around his mind faster than he could process them. Faster than he wanted to try to at least, especially while driving too.

It didn't take long before he pulled into the parking lot and parked. The closest he could get to the door was still a walk to get inside. And he could only hope to find one of those carts she could ride around in.

"Hey, stop brooding. I'll find a scooter then we can get what I need." Jenny poked him in the side, then grinned when he scowled at her.

Seeing her so happy to get out, if even for a trip to the store, made his spirits lift. He pushed his haunting thoughts away and opened his door. He was determined she would have a good time and it was time to make sure of it.

32

Jenny couldn't help the grin that covered her face as Snake pulled the truck back into the parking lot in front of the clubhouse hours later. Tired was an understatement, even though she'd taken it easy, and hadn't even argued about the motorized scooter, no matter how embarrassing it was. It had been worth it to get out and about and to get a little sunshine.

No nothing had been keeping her from going outside and getting sunshine while she'd been here, but she'd done more sleeping than moving around, and even now she felt her bed calling her. But not until they got everything inside and something to eat.

"Are you sure you want to eat here again? I can go pick something up and bring it back. You've been eating nothing but the food here for days. You have to be ready for something different."

She turned and looked at him for a moment. "Are you ready for something different? Are you wanting something in particular?"

"I don't know." He lifted one shoulder and let it drop. "I just thought you might be ready for something more than the limited menu we've got here."

She tilted her head and watched him for a moment. "You know what sounds amazing? Especially if I don't have to go get it?"

"What?"

"Lucky Wishbone."

"Done. Tell me what you want. I'll call in the order then take everything in and go pick it up. Do you want to eat downstairs or in your room?"

"They won't care if we bring in outside food?"

"Not at all," he said with a shake of his head. "The food here is so we have something decent to eat, and to keep our prospects busy when we don't have something else for them to do. It's not to earn money. They don't care if we bring food in, and the prospects usually see it as something they don't have to cook. What do you want?" He pulled out his phone and looked up at her, expectantly.

She gave him her order then opened her door and started maneuvering to get out. Before she'd quite made it, Snake appeared on her side of the truck. He pulled the crutches from behind her seat then waited while she made her way down.

"Go on ahead. I'll bring this stuff in." He started pulling her purchases from the rear seat. "Go ahead and have a seat. I'll take this up to your room then go pick up our dinner."

"Are you sure? I can help carry stuff in." She wasn't sure how she'd manage it, but she would if he said he wanted help.

"I've got it. You go in and get comfortable." He continued to gather bags.

Jenny watched him for another moment then hobbled inside, wrestling with the door for a moment but managing, then made her way to the table she'd started to think of as theirs. By the time she'd gotten settled, the new guy, she tried to remember his name, it was something weird, she knew but couldn't recall what she'd been told this morning, stood next to the table.

"What can I get for you?"

"A soda and a glass of water please."

"No problem. Anything for Snake?" he asked.

She glanced toward the stairs where Snake had just reached the top.

"I'm sure he'll want something, but I'm not sure what. Besides, he's going to run an errand before joining me and I don't want it to get warm. We'll hold off on his drink until he gets back."

"All right. Do you want dinner?"

Jenny shook her head. "That's the errand he's going to run. Pick up dinner." She couldn't help but give him an apologetic smile. "Sorry, I was just ready for something different. It's not a criticism of your cooking, I haven't even tried it yet."

"No worries, we all need a change sometimes. I'll be right back with these." He lifted the small pad he'd been using for notes before turning and leaving.

A few minutes later Snake came back down the stairs, and she watched as he left. The new guy, whose name she still couldn't recall, brought her drink, and left again. She sipped her drink and watched the few men who were here move around and chat with each other while she waited.

"Did he abandon you?" a deep voice far closer than it should be made her turn to spot Sadist approaching.

"Snake? No. he went to go pick up dinner."

"You didn't go with him?"

"We were out most of the afternoon and just got back," she said with a shake of her head. "I was tired, so he volunteered to go pick up food."

He nodded slowly and changed the subject. "How are you feeling?"

"Not too bad. Tired a lot, but I'm improving. Though I can't get rid of this soon enough to suit me." She knocked her knuckles against the brace she had resting in another chair pulled close.

"I bet. Have you been seen since you got released?"

Jenny frowned. That was a silly question. "Of course. I come down every day to eat."

"No. I mean by a medical professional."

"Oh." She felt stupid for not getting that right away when he'd asked. "No. I hadn't even left the building until today."

"Not a problem." He pulled a phone from his pocket and started tapping on the screen. "I think tonight's Kinard's night off. I'll have him swing by, just to make sure everything is on track."

Jenny could only blink and stare at him in surprise. They had their own doctor? The name was a little familiar, but she had a hard time placing it.

"Feel free to have a seat." She motioned to the unused chairs at the table.

According to the patch on the leather vest he wore, this was the club vice president. She should probably stand but didn't have the energy to struggle to her feet at the moment. Inviting him to sit was the best she could think of.

"You sure you don't mind?"

"Not at all. I've wanted to get to know Chuy's friends for a while. This wasn't quite what I had in mind, but you've all been so helpful. Especially since I didn't want to call him home and ruin his honeymoon. Thank you for that."

Sadist lifted one shoulder and let it fall. "We take care of family, and as Gizmo's sister, you're family, even if we didn't know you well until now. Do you know when he's due back?"

"Not for a few more days."

"What do you plan to do once he's home?"

"I'm not sure. I haven't thought about it that much. I should probably go home." The clubhouse door opened, she turned and looked but it was someone she didn't recognize, not Snake. She turned back to Sadist.

He lifted one brow and watched her for a moment. "How do you think your brother will feel about that? You injured and needing help to do day-to-day things and home alone?"

She let her shoulders droop and her head fall. "He'll come stay with me or have me stay with him and Jill." She didn't want either. She didn't want to take Chuy away from Jill or be the third wheel in the newlyweds house. She wasn't sure which option would be worse, only that she didn't want either.

"That's about how I see it." Sadist's voice was gentle. "Is that what you want? If not, you're welcome to stay here until you're getting around better or I'm sure Snake would go with you to your place." He held up one hand to stop her as she started to argue. "We considered sending someone home with you when you were first hurt. It comes with its own set of complications."

"I'd have to pull him from his job, and I'm sure we'd get tired of each other if he was stuck with me twenty-four/seven."

"That's true. We also didn't want you to feel like a stranger, or several, had invaded your home. There were some advantages to keeping you here. And someone was there all the time, plus an element of privacy was only part of it. Ready access to someone to cook for you was a contributing factor." He tilted his head toward where the new guy whose name she still couldn't remember was busy behind the bar pouring drinks for some of the other men scattered around the room. "I'm not saying you need to make a decision right now, or even today. But start thinking about it. Consider too that Gizmo's not going to be happy we kept the truth about how bad you were hurt from him. We did it because it was your choice, but he's going to have an opinion about it, and it likely won't be a quiet one. You need to think about how you want to deal with that. He's our brother, but we backed your decision because we thought it was a good one and we'll help take some of his wrath for it."

Jenny let her head fall until she stared down at her lap for several long seconds. "I'm sorry. I didn't mean to put you all in this position."

"Hey." Sadist waited for her to look up at him. "I'm not telling you this to make you feel bad. I'm trying to make sure you're prepared. If you start thinking about some of this now, you'll have a better idea what to say and how to react. You knew he wouldn't be happy that you didn't call him home. Now think about how to deal with him pissed off."

Jenny nodded and sat up straighter, flexing her neck and back as she did. He was right. She'd known Chuy would be pissed that she didn't tell him how bad it was and have him come home. She'd been willing to deal with it so he could enjoy his honeymoon without worrying about her. Now she had to figure out how to deal with him.

The door opened again and without thinking about it, she turned to see if it was Snake. She couldn't help the grin that spread across her face when he stepped inside, a large take-out bag in one hand. Heat spread through her as he closed the distance to the table where she sat.

"You trying to steal my girl?" Snake lifted one brow at Sadist as he set the food on the table and opened the bag. "Do I need to call Beth and have her tighten your leash?"

Warmth and a sense of contentment she couldn't explain filled her at Snake's calling her his girl.

Sadist rolled his eyes. "I was just keeping her company and talking to her about when Gizmo gets back. Geeze. You act like I was trying to carry her off back to my cave." He pushed himself to his feet. "But now that you're here and have food," he nodded to the bag Snake was busy unpacking, "I'll leave the two of you." Sadist looked back to her. "Think about what I said."

Jenny nodded. "I will. Thank you."

The older man left, Snake put a food box in front of her and another in front of the chair Sadist hadn't been sitting in, then sat.

"What was that all about?" he asked as he opened the box in front of him.

"He was just checking on me. I think he was also keeping me company while you were gone. He did say something about having someone take a look at my leg soon." She watched the older man, wondering what his motive had really been. Had it been just to check on her? Jenny opened her own box of food and popped a fry into her mouth.

Snake frowned. "Is that all?"

"He asked when Chuy would be back and what my plans are for after." She didn't get a chance to say more before he scowled.

"Did he try to get you to go home?" Snake clearly wasn't happy with the idea.

"Actually, the opposite. He encouraged me to stay here after Chuy got back, asking if I wanted to have Chuy stay with me or stay with the newlyweds." She scrunched her nose, as neither idea appealed to her. "I don't like either idea. As much as I want to go home, staying here, at least for a while, is the best option."

Snakes' brows shot up and he looked across the room at where Sadist stood, deep in conversation with another brother Jenny didn't know.

She didn't wait for more questions, but dug into her dinner. The steak fingers were to die for, but something she didn't indulge in often. Tonight, they were a treat she couldn't wait to taste. Kind of like the man sitting across the table from her.

33

"You sit there and tell me where you want things," Snake said once they made it up to her room for the evening. Jenny wanted to put away the things they'd purchased that day, but he didn't want a repeat of the day before.

"I can do it."

"I know you can. But you've done enough today. And there's no reason I can't help."

She shot him an unhappy look but gave him directions on where to put things and before long they had it all put away and the room neat again.

"Now what?" she asked as he pushed the last drawer closed.

"We can watch a little TV if you'd like." He motioned to the TV above her head. They'd have to sit together on the bed to see it, but he was okay with that.

"We can, but I'd rather get to know you a little better." She pushed herself to her feet, picked up the crutches and moved to the bed. "Come sit with me. We can talk."

He watched her for a moment thinking about how once he climbed onto the bed with her, he wouldn't want to get up and there were a few things he'd need before morning. "You get comfortable, I'm going to go to my room and get a few things, so I don't have to leave later. I'll be right back."

"Don't take too long."

"I won't. Not with you here waiting for me." He left, pulling her door closed behind him, then he hurried to his own room and gathered the things he'd need. Clean clothes for tomorrow, an extra charger so they could charge both phones, and a couple other extras. He was on his way back to her room when something popped into his head and he stopped by the supply closet and grabbed a box of condoms, just in case.

He wouldn't be suggesting it, but after the one night he'd spent in her bed, he wouldn't be surprised if she did and the last thing he wanted was to be caught without. Snake stuffed the box in the bundle of clothes in his arms so she wouldn't see it and start pushing, and turned for her room, stopping just in time to keep from running into Kinard.

The biker who was also a nurse and took care of most of the club's medical needs lifted both brows and gave Snake a pointed look, then glanced at the closet, then the pile of clothes in his arms then back to Snake. His brother didn't have to say anything, the look said it for him. Snake didn't know what to say. He wasn't going to defend himself, and it wasn't that he was planning to need them, he just wanted to be prepared.

"Sadist wants me to check on Jenny. He said you've been taking care of her." Kinard gave the bundle of clothes another pointed look. "I don't think Deanna will like if I take care of her like you have been."

Snake scowled but bit back the retort on the tip of his tongue. He wanted to make sure Jenny was okay and pissing off of the person who would check on her and know if she needed something wasn't the way to do that.

"I'm headed back in there. Come this way." Snake led the medic back to Jenny's door, where he knocked, then opened the door a crack. "You decent? There's someone here to see you."

"Come on in," Jenny called back without delay, as if she trusted that anyone he brought to see her would be someone she wanted to see.

Snake pushed the door open, stepped inside and out of the way. "This is Kinard. He's the club medic," he said in introduction as the other man followed him in and closed the door. "Kinard, this is Jenny."

"Hi." Jenny gave a finger wave from where she sat on the bed, her braced leg stretched out in front of her.

"Nice to meet you again. I believe we were introduced at the wedding. I also saw you in the emergency room, though I don't expect you to remember that. you were a bit out of it."

Jenny's face flushed. "I'm sorry. I met so many people that day, most of the faces have blurred together."

"Not a problem. It's not like you've had a traumatic experience since then either." Kinard's friendly smile and easy manner seemed to put Jenny at ease, making Snake just a little less irritated with him.

"Kinard's here to check on you and your leg and make sure everything is going all right. I'm going to put my things away." He motioned to the bathroom. "But if you need anything, say something. I'll hear you."

"I also want to take a look at the incision on your head. How's it been feeling?" Kinard asked.

She met his gaze and nodded then turned her attention to Kinard. "My head's a little itchy but otherwise it feels fine. Sadist said he was going to send someone to check on me, I take it you're it?"

Snake stepped into the bathroom and put his toothbrush on the counter, then the condoms in the drawer. Soft sounds of talking came through the doorway and he did his best not to eavesdrop. He debated hanging his clothes up in here but decided they could go on the dresser or in a drawer. If Jenny wanted a moment's privacy, she would tell him, he was sure.

Pushing the door open, he went back into the bedroom and set his stack of clothes on top of the dresser before going to one of the chairs and sitting. Kinard asked her several questions, poked, and pressed on several spots. Snake could see her clenching her jaw to keep from crying out and was about to call a stop to the exam as it was hurting Jenny too much when the club medic leaned back and met her gaze.

"You seem to be healing well. At least so far. You need to be careful not to overdo it and set your recovery back, but something tells me that one doesn't let that happen if he can help it." Kinard tilted the top of his head toward Snake, letting him know that his return to the room hadn't gone unnoticed. "I won't tell you what you can and can't do, but I want you to be careful not to put too much strain on this leg." Kinard laid a gentle hand on the brace holding the bones in her lower leg in place. "It looks like this incision is doing great and swelling has gone down enough we can put a cast on any time. Do you want to go in and have that done? Or I can bring the stuff for one in and do it here, if you would like?"

She watched him in silence for a moment then narrowed her eyes at Kinard.

"The doc I work for is a specialist, we don't see a lot of broken bones. Walk me though the advantages of a cast over the brace."

"The most obvious is that it's lighter and makes it easier for you to get around, sleep, pretty much everything. Additionally, it's more stable. Less likely for the bones to shift out of place while healing. There are other advantages, but those are the main ones."

She watched him a moment longer then nodded.

"Okay. I could go in, but I hate to ask anyone to take me. Would you mind doing it here?" She'd finished asking before Snake could speak up and say he wouldn't mind taking her.

"Not at all. I'll make sure I have the stuff and see you tomorrow. I've got a shift in the afternoon. How does morning work for you?"

Jenny laughed. "Any time works for me. It's not like I'm running off to keep up with a hopping social schedule. I didn't even do that when I had two good legs."

A wry smile carved one side of Kinard's mouth. "Be patient. Give it a few weeks and you'll be up and running again. Then you'll wish you had the excuse of a bum leg to take it easy."

"I don't know. I feel like I'm about to go out of my mind. I'm used to being up and going and doing." She glanced over at Snake. "Come keep me company," Jenny said in what was probably the most demanding tone he'd ever heard her use, as she patted the bed beside herself. "You said we could talk. I don't want to feel like I'm yelling everything."

"I'll join you in just a minute. I wanted to stay out of the way while he checked you out, then get anything you might want before we settle in for a while." Snake felt Kinard's gaze on him, and the other man's knowledge of the condoms he'd picked up. Both felt heavier than they should.

Ten minutes later, Kinard gone, and the door closed behind him, Snake turned to watch Jenny. "I would have taken you to get a cast put on."

"I know, but I didn't want to take you away from whatever you might have going on."

"Sweetheart, all I have going on is work, the occasional errand for the club and spending time with you and to my mind, I don't get nearly enough of that last one."

34

Jenny smiled as warmth spread through her at his words. He wanted to spend more time with her. She didn't mind, because she wanted to spend more time with him too.

"Tell me more about you." She shifted, trying to get more comfortable. She couldn't wait until they replaced this stupid brace with the cast tomorrow. Maybe it would be easier to get around then. She could only hope it would make it easier to sleep, shower, and maybe get out of the clubhouse more often. That made her think of how close the shop where Snake worked was. Maybe without the weight of the brace she could go over there for a bit. It would help her get some sunshine and just out of the clubhouse for a while.

"What do you want to know?"

She couldn't tell if he was being accommodating or avoiding the subject.

"Where did you grow up?"

"Small town in central Texas that I'm sure you've never heard of."

"What makes you think that?"

"Sweetheart, most people in Texas have never heard of it, much less people from two states away. Let's just say it's little more than a wide spot in the road and I got away as soon as I could."

She frowned. "What about your family?" It might have just been her and Chuy for years, but they relied on each other, at least she relied on him.

"Don't have any left." He gave his head a brief shake. "Mom got sick when I was in high school. Cancer. She lost her battle my senior year. That's when I enlisted. There was nothing left to hold me there."

"What about your dad?" She couldn't help the frown that creased her brow.

"Never knew him. He took off before I was born."

"I'm sorry." She picked up his hand and held it, not sure if she did it for him or herself. She loved having him close and she still missed her parents, even though they'd been gone almost five years now. She couldn't imagine never knowing one of them. She had so many questions, but didn't know what to ask, what might hurt.

"It's been a long-time, sweetheart, and it's hard to miss what you never knew. But I do still miss Mama. She'd have liked you." He squeezed her hand briefly, then eased the grip and met her gaze.

"Oh? What makes you say so?" She tilted her head and watched him, wondering if thinking about his mama caused the ache deep in his chest that thinking about her own parents caused in hers.

"You're smart, independent, and have a heart as big as Texas." His hand squeezed hers again, making her look up at him and bringing her mind back to what he was saying instead of the loss of her own parents.

"She valued independence?"

"She raised a wild, smart assed kid all on her own. Independence was big to Mama. As was loyalty, integrity, and honor. All of which I can tell you have in spades." He leaned in and dropped a quick kiss to the end of her nose.

Jenny frowned, wondering what had made him decide she was loyal. She was, but what made him see it?

"So you enlisted... Navy, right?"

"Yep, Navy." He looked away and she wondered a moment what he was thinking.

She couldn't help but notice the pride in his voice and the way he sat up just a little straighter as he said the one word. That didn't surprise her. From what she'd seen, no matter what branch of the military a person joined, they were proud of it and fiercely defensive of why they believed it was the superior branch.

"Navy? From Texas? What made you go Navy?" She had no quarrel with any branch, but it seemed an odd choice. She shifted again, finding the way the brace pulled on her lower leg making it difficult to sit in one position for long.

"I wanted to get as far as I could from home, and being from the plains of Texas, that seemed like something on the water. At least to a depressed eighteen-year-old."

He was quiet for a moment, and she thought he was through talking, at least until she asked another question. She wondered if maybe she should change the subject, then he spoke again.

"I have no regrets. I learned a lot and I have a good life and a family I wouldn't turn my back on for anything now, but I've wondered a few times. If I had it all to do over again, knowing what I know now, if I wouldn't do it different. I'm glad I don't have that choice. While there are a few things I might choose differently on, now I'm afraid a different choice might land me somewhere different. And I don't want to be anywhere but where I am right now." He picked up her hand and kissed the back of it, meeting her gaze for the first time in a bit, and held it.

Heat pooled in her belly as she realized he meant that literally. He wanted to be here, with her, right now. He had no where he'd rather be.

She waited until he lowered her hand back to the bed between them then she leaned in, stretched up and brushed her mouth against his.

"I'm pretty good with where we are now too. Though I can think of somewhere I would rather be."

"Where's that?" His voice was barely more than a whisper, but they were so close she had no trouble hearing.

"In your arms and without this stupid thing." She rapped the knuckles of one hand against her brace.

35

Jenny's words of the only place she could think of better than where she was right now was in his arms sent a bolt of panic through him, but it was quickly followed by a warmth he didn't want to stop. Ever. Not if he could help it.

"I can't do anything about the brace, at least not yet, but I can do something about the rest of that. Come here, let's get comfortable." He scooted closer to where she sat, leaning against the wall at the head of the bed and lifted his arm so she could lean against him. When she did, he wrapped his arm around her shoulder, then closed his eyes and inhaled. Her light, floral scent washed over him, triggering something deep inside that had him relaxing against her. "You want to talk about something else, watch something or just sit like this a while?" He motioned to the TV on the far wall with his free hand.

"I don't care. I can't think of any other questions, but I don't watch much TV. What do you like?"

"Sweetheart, I usually turn on the TV for a little noise while I'm doing something else, like making dinner or working on something, then it's usually something like the news or sports since you don't have to watch every time to know what's going on. Occasionally I'll turn on a movie if I'm looking for a distraction."

She turned and watched him for a moment, her expression said she was considering his words.

"What kind of movies do you like?"

"Mostly action flicks. I like car chases and shoot-em-up scenes." He didn't want to admit his love for juvenile comedies. Not that he meant kid's stuff, he hadn't seen any of that in years. No, he liked teenage dumb comedy. It was an old film, but one of his favorite movies was *Dumb and Dumber*. Yes, he knew it was stupid, but to him it was so stupid it was funny, even the millionth time he saw it. He wasn't quite ready to let her see that side of him. Though if she stayed around long, she'd figure it out.

"What's on the movie channels? Or streaming services? We can probably find a movie if nothing else." Jenny's voice brought him back to what they were doing and away from his thoughts about what he didn't want her to find out.

"Let's take a look, there are several movie channels." He turned the TV on and found the guide and navigated so they could find out what was on.

Jenny snuggled closer to his side, shifting a bit to get comfortable, then laying her head on his shoulder. Warmth spread through him and in that moment, he knew he'd watch anything she wanted, as long as she stayed just like that. He never wanted to let her go. Never wanted to let anything hurt her or take her from him.

⚜ ⚜

"**W**hat the hell is going on here?"

The shouted words, along with the sound of the door bouncing off the wall, woke Snake with a jerk. He reached for a pistol on the nightstand that wasn't there as he spun to face the threat, making sure to put Jenny at his back, so he was between her and whatever was coming through the door.

"What the hell, Chuy? I was asleep." Jenny's voice was rough with sleep. "Go away and let me get dressed. I'll be out in a few minutes."

Gizmo's gaze swept over first his sister, then hardened as it moved to Snake.

"I'll wait for you, but him. He's coming with me." Gizmo stabbed a finger in Snake's direction.

"No. He's not. I need him to help me get moving. We'll join you downstairs in a few minutes. Now close the door and go away." There was no sleep left in her voice as she told her brother to leave them alone.

Snake felt the bed shift and knew she was moving. Gizmo might be pissed and might hurt him, but he was also Snake's brother and wouldn't kill him. Jenny, on the other hand, had a hard time getting moving first thing in the morning, so he turned to see what she was doing. She was sitting up, the blanket and sheet pooled in her lap. Snake could only be thankful he hadn't let her talk him into stripping down to the skin the night before. He was in his shorts while she wore an oversized t-shirt and loose shorts.

She flung the blanket back and with a grimace, tried to swing the brace off the edge of the bed to get up.

"Let me." Snake ignored the open door and his brother still standing there, scowling at him as he moved around the bed to help her with the brace.

"What the fuck, Jenny?" Gizmo's words reminded her he hadn't left like she'd told him to, and she glared up at him.

"I told you to go away. We will meet you downstairs. Go order me some breakfast and coffee if you insist on babying me. I need some caffeine."

"What the fuck?" Gizmo repeated.

This time Jenny didn't say anything but twisted around and pinned her brother with a glare that made him cringe. He left, closing the door behind him.

"Ten minutes. If you're not downstairs in ten minutes, I'm coming back up." His voice carried through the door.

Jenny rolled her eyes. "He will too, not that I care. It's not like he caught us in the act. But still." She took a deep breath and let it out slowly before looking up and meeting Snake's gaze. "Thanks for not freaking out when he burst in like that." She leaned close and dropped a brief kiss on his lips then pulled back. "Help me get ready, will you? He wasn't kidding about ten minutes." She winced as she tried again to slide the brace off the edge of the bed. "I won't miss this thing."

"You won't have to deal with it much longer." He helped her into the bathroom, then pulled on his jeans, snagged his t-shirt before grabbing her crutches and giving them to her.

"What do you want to wear?" He looked at her expectantly.

"Just a pair of shorts. They'll be the easiest to get on. It might be a little cool, but the shorts will make it easier to trade this thing in for the cast too." She moved to the table and sat. "I don't care what shirt, just grab me something."

Snake pulled a pair of shorts from the drawer and held them up. "How are these?"

Jenny shook her head. "Not those. They're too tight. Look for the blue pair."

He turned back to the drawer, a frown creasing his brow as he looked for the pair she wanted. It took a moment, but after a moment he lifted a second pair for her approval.

"Yes."

He passed her the clothing, and went back to looking for a top for her. He knew she didn't want to go downstairs in the t-shirt she slept in.

"How about this one?" He held up a black tank top.

"That's fine, but I need a bra with it. Those are in the drawer above that one."

She bent and began working the shorts up over her foot and the brace that covered the lower half of her right leg.

He opened the drawer and stared down at a jumble of bras and panties.

"Um, which do you want?"

"I don't care. Just grab one."

Snake stared into the drawer for a moment not sure where to start. Overwhelmed, he grabbed one, plucked it free and gave it to her. "This one work?"

"That's fine."

She dropped it on the table while she finished working the shorts over her brace, then it looked like she folded her good leg like a pretzel to get it into the other hole of the shorts then pushed herself to her feet and shimmied her hips as she pulled them up over the ass he wanted to grab and hold onto. He wanted to help her, but knew she wouldn't welcome him stepping in.

He grabbed socks for them both then went to other chair at the table. He pulled on his socks and boots while she shed her t-shirt, put on the bra, and tank top. When he finished with his boots, he went to his knees in front of her and took care of her shoe, so she wouldn't have to struggle with it.

"Want help with your hair?"

"How bad is it?" She smoothed a hand over it.

"Not bad. The braid held up pretty well. It's just a little frizzy."

"Then let's just leave it. I don't want to deal with it right now." She glanced at the clock next to the bed, then sighed. "We might as well go down. He wasn't kidding about that time limit. If we take too long, he'll be back up here beating down the door."

Snake glanced over at the door, as if he'd heard someone on the other side. He hadn't. And he didn't want to go down and have to admit to his brother that he'd fallen for the other man's sister, but he also wasn't going to let her go down and face him alone. No. This was the right thing to do, so he would.

He stood and offered her a hand. Once she'd let him pull her to her feet, he made sure she had her crutches then opened the door. They went through the usual routine of her going ahead while he locked the door, this time he wished they locked the door while inside, but had gotten in the habit of only locking it when they were gone. He followed, picking up her crutches at the top of the stairs where she'd left them while she made her way down, and following with them.

At the base of the stairs, she looked around while she waited for him to bring her crutches, presumably looking for Gizmo. She didn't have long to wait because Snake was only a couple steps behind her.

He didn't think she'd spotted Gizmo, because he hadn't, and once she was able to move away from the stairs, she went to the table that had become theirs and sat. Snake pulled the chair she rested her brace on close and helped her lift her leg up into it. He straightened to find Gizmo standing beside him. He opened his mouth to greet his friend, but before he could get a word out, Gizmo's fist collided with his jaw with a loud smack that set Snake's ears ringing.

"Hey, what the hell was that for?" Jenny's voice made him step between her and Gizmo before he could shake his head and focus. Something hard stopped him.

Snake glanced down to find Jenny using one of her crutches to push her brother away from Snake. He shook his head and fought back the grin that his woman would defend him even when she wasn't at one hundred percent, and against her brother. But she shouldn't have to.

"I probably deserved that, so I'll let you have that one, but not again. It hurt like hell, but worse than that, it upsets Jenny."

"She's my sister and I found you in bed with her. Why the hell is she here and not home anyway? I assume this is from the accident? Why wasn't I told how bad she was hurt?" Gizmo was shouting by the time he finished.

36

Jenny stared up at her brother, wondering what bug had crawled up his ass and died.

"Stop acting like an idiot. Sit down and we'll talk."

Chuy shot another glare at Snake, then reached for a chair. Before he could pull it out, she hooked the rail along the bottom with her good foot, keeping him from being able to pull it away from the table. He tugged for a moment then looked at her, obviously unhappy.

"Since you were so kind in how you woke me up, I think you owe me some caffeine." Jenny pasted on her sweetest smile, or at least the sweetest one she could manage having been awake less than ten minutes.

"Let the prospect bring you whatever you want." Her brother's words were little more than snarled.

"He'll bring my breakfast, because I'll ask him nicely, but you have not been nice, not to me or Snake and you need a moment to remember your manners. You'll bring us both some coffee, or you can go sit over there," she waved toward the couches arranged in front of several TVs in the corner, "until you remember how to talk to civilized people."

Chuy glared at her for a moment. "I'm not waiting on the asshole who seduced my sister as soon as my back was turned."

"Do you really think so little of me?" She glared right back. "Go get the drinks and get something for you while you're there. Maybe something that will sweeten your disposition.

Because right now you're dangerously close to having to pick your ass up off the floor." She wasn't sure how she would manage it with only one good foot and iffy balance, but if her brother kept pushing her, she'd find a way. Since it wouldn't be the first time she knocked him down, he had no reason to doubt she wouldn't again. He continued to glare at her for several seconds, until she lifted one brow, silently daring him to cross her.

Chuy spun on one heel and stomped away muttering something under his breath that sounded suspiciously like bitchy headstrong women.

Jenny turned to Snake. "You all right?" She reached for him, even though she knew she couldn't reach his jaw to check him out while seated.

"I'm fine. He just surprised me." Snake glanced in her brother's direction. "Are you sure sending him for drinks for us is the best idea?"

"Yeah, it will give him a minute to think and remember I'm an adult and make my own decisions. Come sit next to me." She reached for the chair opposite the one where her leg rested and tugged it till it was close enough, she could hold his hand or lay her hand on his leg if she wanted.

With one last glance toward Chuy, he came around the table and sat.

"What do you want me to tell him?" he asked.

"Leave him to me." She patted his leg then took his hand in hers and wove their fingers together.

Snake shot her a frown that clearly said he didn't like the idea. She hoped he would at least let her try before he stepped in. On impulse, she leaned over and kissed him, lingering for a moment with her lips on his because he wasn't reacting. He wasn't kissing her back, but after a moment he gave in and opened his mouth to hers. He brought one hand up to cup her jaw and Jenny soon lost track of where they were and what was going on around them. All that mattered at that moment was the two of them.

A throat clearing, what sounded like inches away, reminded Jenny of where they were and what they'd been doing. Waiting for Chuy. She pulled her lips away from Snake and turned to find her brother standing next to the table, a glass of soda and two cups of coffee in his hands and a scowl marring his face.

"I'd really like it if you would remember where you are and that she's my sister." Chuy's words were aimed at Snake, as was his scowl. He set down the glass in front of the chair she'd been holding onto, then a mug of coffee in front of her and Snake before pulling out the chair she no longer held with her foot.

Snake held up his free hand in surrender, as if he wanted Chuy to see he was unarmed. She didn't even have to tighten her fingers in his to keep him from releasing it. With a quick squeeze to let him know she appreciated that, she looked at Chuy, one brow lifted.

"And if I'm the one who started it?"

His face turned red then he closed his eyes and took several deep breaths. She watched as the muscles in his jaw flexed and bulged. He might be mad, but he knew better than to rip into her like he had Snake.

She thought he was about to speak when Savage approached the table.

"I see you've already got drinks, but I brought this," he set the small dish of coffee additives in front of her, "what can I get you for breakfast?"

She couldn't help but turn a smile to the prospect. They spent a couple of minutes discussing options before she let him know what she wanted. Snake put in his order, then they all turned to look at Chuy.

"What?" he asked through clenched teeth. He obviously hadn't been following what was going on at the table.

"Do you want something to eat?" Jenny reminded herself he was being civil, she could do the same, even if he was being an idiot.

A startled look crossed his face as he looked up and met Savage's gaze. "No. Sorry. I've already eaten. I'm good with this."

Jenny waited while Savage left then turned to her brother.

"You're back early, is something wrong? Is Jill okay?"

"Jill's fine. There was a storm moving in and they evacuated all the tourists from the island. Claimed we'd be safer that way. Imagine my surprise when I stopped by your place to surprise you and found the place locked up and empty." Chuy shot her a frown. "Then I come over here to see if anyone's heard from you and find what's left of your car next door. That accident was a hell of a lot worse than I was told about." He looked back and forth between the two of them. "I get inside and ask the first person I ran across," he jerked his thumb toward the kitchen door where Savage had gone to fix their breakfast, "if anyone knew where you were. He did. He even told me which room... He didn't say you weren't alone." His frown turned to a scowl as he pinned Snake with a threatening look.

"Don't blame him. I'm the one who decided I didn't want you to know how bad it was," Jenny said while doctoring her coffee with the things Savage had brought. Chuy's gaze flicked back to her, and she continued. "I didn't want to ruin your honeymoon." She sighed, knowing it was time to come clean, at least about the accident. "I was t-boned. I didn't realize how bad it was at the scene, but I knew I didn't want you to come home early. I called the number you gave me in case I needed anything while you were gone." She paused to take a sip of her coffee. She used the chance to watch her brother for a moment, trying to gauge his mood.

"Snake showed up on the scene before they took me to the hospital. He said he was there to get my car, but I think he was checking on me too." She squeezed his hand where their fingers were still woven together and sitting in his lap. "A lot of the rest of that day is a bit of a blur. But I know there were people at the hospital for me, even if they didn't let me see them for long." She looked away, glancing down at the leg still in the brace stretched out in front of her. "I ended up having to have surgery, partly because I had a bleed that they had to relieve the pressure on." She reached up and touched the lobe of the ear the incision from that sat behind, but remembered not to touch the incision. They'd taken the bandage off and she didn't want to risk getting it dirty or infected. Then she lowered her hand to her right leg and touched the brace. "And to set my leg, but the swelling was too bad for a cast, and I ended up with this instead." She knocked on the rim of the brace with one fist. "Snake was there when I woke up and never left while I was in the hospital."

Chuy opened his mouth, and she didn't know what he was about to say, but she needed to get this all out. So she held up one hand in a stop signal and continued to talk.

"They offered to call you home right away and several other times. From the scene, when I woke from surgery and before I was released. I refused. I didn't want to ruin your honeymoon and there was nothing wrong that wouldn't heal." She broke off long enough for a long drink from her coffee. She closed her eyes for a moment and waited for the caffeine to hit her brain. "I wanted to go home. I insisted I would be okay and that I could handle things on my own. Sadist flat out refused. He said I could go home, but I wouldn't be alone. He would have someone with me all the time or I could stay here at the clubhouse."

Chuy started to speak again but she interrupted him.

"Let me finish, please."

He didn't say anything, but crossed his arms over his chest, waiting.

"He told me I could have a room of my own here, but there would always be someone around. I didn't see much choice, and as much as I resented it at the time, I decided here was the lesser of two evils. Now though, I'm glad I chose to stay here. Even with the stairs it's been easier here. There's someone to make sure I eat, someone who will come immediately if I need anything, and no one comes into my room unless I invite them." She squeezed Snake's hand again before falling silent and waiting for her brother's recriminations.

"Then how did I find the two of you in bed? You're hurt, he has no business seducing my little sister."

Snake opened his mouth to defend her, but Jenny squeezed his fingers, and he closed it, though she didn't miss the way his jaw flexed as he clenched his teeth.

"There's so much wrong with that statement I don't know where to start. Let me just jump into the middle. Number one. You burst in while we were sleeping. SLEEPING. And in case you didn't notice, we had clothes on. Number two. I'm a big girl. I decide who I sleep with and who I don't, not you." She stretched her good leg under the table and bumped his leg with her toe, not so subtly reminding him of how she used to kick him in the shins when he'd pissed her off. She hadn't done it in a couple years, but she wasn't above doing it again if he continued to act like an idiot.

37

It had been Snake's first instinct to jump to Jenny's defense. It didn't matter that Gizmo was her brother. Snake didn't like the way he talked to her.

But he couldn't help but smile at the fire in her voice as she told him off. She didn't need him to defend her. She didn't hesitate to do it herself. A self-sufficient woman, one who could let someone else take care of her when the time was right? Well, Snake wasn't sure there was anything hotter.

He watched the exchange between the siblings, realizing how hard he'd fallen for her. If he had his way, she'd never have to face anything hard again, or at least not alone. He wasn't foolish enough to believe that life wouldn't have times that were more difficult than others, but he wanted to be there with her because he knew from experience that difficult things were easier to handle if you had someone to share the load.

"What about you?" Gizmo's voice pulled him from his thoughts.

"What about me what?"

The club tech sergeant glared at him. Jenny squeezed his hand.

"He's asking your intentions toward me, babe." She sounded more amused than anything else, so Snake glanced at her, and sure enough she was smiling at him.

"What do you want me to tell him?" he asked her, ignoring the man across the table from them.

She lifted one shoulder and let it fall.

"Whatever you want. I already told him what's between you and me isn't any of his business."

Damn. Snake wished he'd been paying attention for that. He turned his attention back to Gizmo and found the man's face red and his jaw bulging. Clearly, he wasn't happy with their ignoring him or his sister's responses.

"I ought to tell you that what happens between Jenny and me is none of your business." Snake fought the urge to wince at the sound of Gizmo's teeth grinding together. "But I'm not that much of an ass." He paused, watching the tech sergeant for a couple of moments, enjoying the feeling of Jenny beside him, her hand in his. "I'm also not going to tell you exactly what's between us. That's our business and frankly more than a little creepy for a brother to ask about." He couldn't help the grin that spread across his face as Gizmo's face went even more red. Sometimes it was hard to resist the urge to screw with his brothers.

After a couple of seconds, he took mercy on Gizmo and spoke again. "Honestly though, man. I don't know where this is headed. But I can promise you I'm not taking advantage of her. I genuinely like Jenny and I'm doing my best to take care of her, at least as much as she'll let me."

For the first time since they'd sat down, the corner of Gizmo's mouth quirked upward, as if he understood how stubborn and independent his sister could be.

"We're not holding her hostage here. She's been given the option to go home, but not alone. We weren't going to leave her to struggle with her recovery and possibly hurt herself because she was all alone." Snake glanced over at Jenny and found her rolling her eyes at him. "She's smart, but also a bit more stubborn than is good for her."

"How much longer?" Gizmo's tone wasn't as angry or aggressive, but had turned more begrudging.

"We're not sure yet. Kinard's bringing the stuff by this morning to replace the brace with a cast, then we'll look at things again," Snake said.

"Sadist asked me yesterday if I wanted to take you away from Jill to stay with me or to go stay with the two of you. I don't want either. You two deserve the time to yourselves. Besides, I'm good here. I have a door that locks, food when I want it and if I need help with anything, someone nearby to get me what I need." She didn't release his hand as she reached across the table to cover her brother's with her free hand. "It might not be how you would do things, but I'm good with it. I'm sure I'll go home soon. Not sure how long until I can go back to work yet, but Snake had me check into things, and my short-term disability insurance will pay enough to cover my bills."

"What about your car?" Gizmo asked, lifting one brow. "Have you seen it since the accident?"

Snake remained quiet. He'd taken a look at it, and one of the other men had gone out and taken the pictures her insurance company had requested. He hadn't told her yet because she didn't need one more thing to worry about, not until she needed to, but he was about ninety percent sure they were going to total the car.

That didn't mean the car couldn't be fixed, just that the repairs would cost more than the car was worth, or at least in the insurance company's eyes. He'd planned to talk to her in the next few days about the car, to see how attached to it she was and how important she felt it was to fix it rather than just replace.

"Not up close. I saw it when we pulled up here, and again when we went out yesterday, but other than letting my insurance company know there had been an accident I hadn't thought about it very much. I just wasn't ready to." She sighed. "I guess I'll need to do that soon, to make sure I have a way to get back and forth to work, once I can go back." She picked up her mug and took a drink.

Snake squeezed her hand, hoping to reassure her. "We'll figure it out. I'll take a look at the car and see what we need to do to fix it and if it's even worth it." He wasn't about to go into whether or not she wanted it fixed, not now or in front of her brother but later...

Savage appeared with their breakfast, setting the plates in front of them with a grin.

"I hope you enjoy. Let me top off your drinks." He hurried off before Snake could say anything else.

Jenny closed her eyes and took a deep breath as she released his hand for the first time since sitting down. "These smells divine." She unrolled the flatware from the napkin the prospect had brought with him and dug in.

Snake flexed his aching jaw as he unrolled his own flatware, his gaze staying on Gizmo as he got ready to eat his own breakfast. They remained silent for several minutes, as Savage refreshed their drinks and he and Jenny ate. Snake couldn't help but wonder what Gizmo was thinking, the same for Jenny, but the glaring and animosity seemed to have passed so he let it go.

38

Jenny finished eating and pushed her plate away, before looking back across the table at her brother. She was sorry they'd had to cut their honeymoon short, but was glad to see him. He looked happy. Well, he did now that his anger over how he'd found her and Snake seemed to have passed.

"Other than a storm forcing you to leave early, how was Tahiti? And I assume Jill is at home? Why didn't you bring her along?" Jenny asked, hoping he was ready to let her change the subject. She didn't want to talk about herself any longer. Leaning back in her seat, she dropped her hands into her lap, well one of them. The other she dropped on Snake's leg where she found his hand and wove her fingers in with his. Having him close and just simple contact calmed her.

"It was fun. Not quite what I expected, but we had a great time. And Jill's at home. I was just planning to stop by your place and surprise you. It's turned into a lot more."

"How much of the island did you actually get to see?" Snake asked.

Her brother's face darkened. Jenny tilted her head to watch him. She didn't get to see him embarrassed often, and she found it immensely interesting. Even if he did shoot her a scowl.

"Well, some."

39

Jenny bit the inside of her lip as she tried to keep from laughing out loud. As if she had any idea why Chuy and Jill hadn't seen as much of the exotic vacation destination as they'd hoped. She did hope they'd had a better time than she had. But that wouldn't have been hard, especially with how much time she'd spent alone in that room upstairs.

She glanced up at the railing. Thinking of the time she'd spent up there not alone.

Movement on her hand drew her attention. She turned to look at it and found Snake rubbing his thumb back and forth over the back of her hand, as if he knew what she was thinking and wanted to let her know. She gave him a smile, but resisted the urge to lean in and kiss his cheek. Chuy wasn't ready for it, even if she could think of nothing that sounded better, at least at the moment.

"Sweetheart?" Something in Snake's tone made her glance up at his face.

He caught her eye and tipped the top of his head toward the door. Curious, she followed his gaze and found the medic guy who had checked her over the night before. The one who was going to replace the cursed brace with a cast. She couldn't help the smile that almost seemed to split her face. She would be getting rid of the heavy brace.

At her change of expression, Chuy twisted around to find out what she'd seen. When he saw who had arrived, he turned back to her, a frown marring his brow.

"Do you smile like that for all my brothers now?"

"No. Just the ones who will help me get rid of this thing." She knocked on the brace again. "It's heavy and uncomfortable. I hate it."

Chuy looked at her as if she was being naive. "And you think a cast is going to be better?"

"Maybe not, but at least it won't be so heavy. I'll be able to move around easier and roll over in bed." She closed her eyes and tried to remember what rolling over in bed without struggling with the stupid brace was like. It was a fond memory and hopefully one she'd get to experience again soon.

"You look good," Kinard said as he approached the table, his eyes flicking around to take in everyone seated there. "You ready to do this?" He lifted what looked like a large plastic toolbox he carried in one hand. His gaze flicked down to where her leg was propped on the chair in front of her. "Want to do this here or go upstairs?"

"Here's good with me if it's good with you." Jenny shrugged.

"No problem." The medic guy turned to her brother. "Glad to see you back safe. How was your trip?"

"Great. You need something to do this?" Chuy glanced down at the box the other man still carried.

"I need a good size bowl of warm water. It doesn't need to be hot, but warmer than room temperature. Can you get that while I get started?"

"Sure." Chuy stood and headed for the kitchen.

Once he was gone, Kinard grabbed the back of his chair and turned it toward her leg. "Let's take a look here." Setting the box on the floor beside himself, he flipped the latches and opened it. Then he pulled out and put on a pair of black medical gloves.

"Anything I can do to help?" Snake asked.

"Slide the table out of the way a little but other than that, no. Just sit there with her. This shouldn't hurt, but I need to feel around a little and make sure her bones haven't shifted and need to be reduced again before I can do this."

She glanced at Snake as he released her hand, then stood and slid the table away from where her leg still rested in the chair. When he came back, he scooted his chair closer to hers and sat with his chest up against her side, his arms wrapping around her.

"You won't hurt her, will you?" Snake's voice rumbled through her he sat so close. Between his heat, and the gentle way he held her, she relaxed against him, letting her head fall to rest on his chest, despite keeping her eyes on where the medic's hands gently touched and probed her leg.

"Not if I can help it." Kinard didn't look up from her leg. His hands were gentle as he checked her healing incision then loosened and removed the brace, feeling his way up and down her lower leg, sometimes with his eyes closed as if he was seeing with his hands instead of his eyes. "Okay," he said after a moment. "Everything feels good to go, now we can start with the cast." He bent and pulled several things out of the box, using the lid that hung off the back as a shelf to lay things out.

"This won't take too long, then we'll give it a few minutes to harden and then you can get up and move around." He paused and looked up to meet her gaze. "I still don't want you putting any weight on it for several weeks. You'll still need to use the crutches and stay off it as much as possible, but the cast should be more comfortable than the brace."

Jenny watched as he worked quickly, but with sure fingers that told her he had done this more than a few times before. She relaxed against Snake, wondering exactly how well she'd be able to move around once the cast was on.

39

Snake watched as one of his brothers ran his hands up and down his woman's leg, wishing he could stomp out that spark of jealousy that flared in the pit of his stomach. Kinard was doing his job, not feeling her up. Besides, it was only her calf.

Still, he had to clench his teeth to keep from telling the other man to keep his hands to himself. Forcing himself to look away, Snake scanned the room, making sure there was nothing out of place and no one who wasn't supposed to be there. Not that there ever was, but that was because they all kept an eye out. They all watched out. And with someone as precious to him as the woman leaning against his chest here, he wasn't about to let his guard down.

The door leading to the kitchen swung open, drawing his attention. Gizmo was on his way back with a large bowl.

"How's this?" he asked as he set the bowl, about three quarters full of water on the table beside Kinard.

The medic glanced over then gently pressed his bare forearm to the side of the bowl.

"That's great. Let me just finish up with this." He went back to wrapping a wide cloth up and down Jenny's leg. "Have you ever had a cast before?" he asked Jenny.

"No. I've never broken anything before." Her voice was soft in a way that set off flags in Snake's head.

He glanced up at Gizmo to find a confused frown on her brother's face too. He thought it was strange too. Snake didn't like this, not at all.

He tilted his head and turned to see if he could see her face, but the way she held her head, watching as Kinard continued wrapping the padding around her leg made it impossible to get a good look at her.

"Sweetheart?" He kept his voice soft as he didn't want her to think he was upset or yelling at her.

Jenny didn't respond, look in his direction or give any indication she'd heard him. He repeated himself, a little louder this time but again, got no reaction from her. He frowned and lifted one hand to her chin, with gentle pressure he turned her head to face him? "Sweetheart?"

She blinked and looked at him. "What?"

"Are you okay?"

"Yeah, I'm fine. Why?" A frown creased her brow as she watched him back.

"You seem off. Are you sure you're okay?"

"Yeah. I was just distracted. Watching and thinking."

Snake met her gaze and watched her for a moment, making sure she wasn't hiding something from him then, after a moment he leaned in and placed a soft kiss on her mouth.

The last thing either of them needed was to lose themselves in each other but a soft, chaste kiss should be okay.

He pulled back and searched her face for any sign she was still distracted. A small smile curved her lips, making him go back for another kiss, this one a little longer but no less chaste. There was no tongue, no tasting, just a pressing of their lips together. That didn't stop someone from clearing his throat a few steps away.

Snake ignored him and kept his attention on the woman in his arms. This time, as he pulled away and watched her, a huge grin spread across her face.

"I'd be up to do that again. But can I get a little more you?" The mischievous look in her eye told him she was only half teasing. Snake suspected she'd said it for Gizmo's benefit.

"I need you to keep your leg still, at least for a few more minutes." Kinard's voice held no censor, but was matter of fact.

Snake glanced at the club medic to find his attention on what he was doing, soaking the casting material in the bowl of water Gizmo had brought. Snake had no doubt he'd get the job done as quickly as he could, so he could move on to whatever he had planned next.

"Sorry," Jenny's voice was soft again.

"You're fine," Kinard said, pulling the cast material from the water and turning back to the leg he'd positioned so it was bent at the knee while her foot rested on the seat of the chair in front of him. "Just don't get too distracted and enthusiastic. This won't take but a few minutes more." He started wrapping the black material around the pale padding. After a couple of wraps, he glanced up at Jenny. "Sorry, I would have offered a choice of colors, but all I keep in my kit is black, as that's what the guys tend to want."

"Black's fine." She turned back to the medic still wrapping her leg. "It just makes it harder to decorate."

Snake knew better than that, but he wasn't going to say anything, not now. Instead, he'd surprise her later. Instead, he used the tip of one finger to turn her face back to where he still looked over her shoulder and kissed her again. This time taking his time and lingering as he tasted her. He wasn't sure if watching Kinard put the cast on her leg had reminded her of the accident or something else, but she didn't seem to mind his method of distraction.

After a couple moments, Gizmo cleared his throat again. This time it wasn't Snake who ended the kiss but Jenny who pulled away. She looked embarrassed. Snake didn't like that. He turned and pinned Gizmo with a scowl.

"She's still my sister." Giz scowled back.

"Then turn around or go away." Snake had to work to keep the snarl from his tone. He didn't like that Jenny felt judged for something so tame. "If it was Jill here trying to deal with something like this, wouldn't you do what you could to distract her?"

The crease between Gizmo's brows grew deeper. He threw his hands in the air and spun away. "I'll be back after he's done. I still want to talk to the two of you."

"He doesn't like us together." Jenny sounded unhappy as she stated the obvious.

"He'll get over it," Kinard said without looking up. "You can't live your life to suit your brother. And if you are happy with Snake then eventually, he'll get over that it's his brother and he'll be happy for you too." He finished smoothing the cast material down and looked up at the two of them. "Just give him some time. Speaking of time, this will take ten to fifteen minutes to harden, then you're good to go. Remember to keep it dry and I don't want you to put any weight on it for at least two weeks. I'll check it out again before then." He looked back and forth between the two of them and waited for Jenny's nod of understanding before he pinned Snake with a serious look. "I wasn't kidding that Gizmo will get over it. Unless you do something stupid and hurt her. Then you know him, he'll find somewhere to hide the body where it will never be found." He stood and his gazed flicked to Jenny. "Stay here, let that harden while I take care of this." He picked up the bowl Gizmo had brought and carried it back into the kitchen.

"Did he just threaten you?" Jenny looked up at him with an uncertain expression.

"Yes and no." He kissed the top of her nose to reassure her. "He was trying to be reassuring but warning at the same time. That's okay though."

"Why? How is it okay that he threatened you?" She looked confused.

"Because we'd do the same for any sister of any brother. I understand where they're coming from, both of them. And the last thing I'm going to do is hurt you." Snake couldn't help but lift one corner of his mouth in a wry smile. "Well, I'll amend that. I'm sure once in a while, not intending to, I'll manage to hurt your feelings. That's kind of the way things go in life. But I'll never intentionally hurt you and I'll never physically hurt you. You know that, right?"

"I never thought you'd hurt me. If I did, I wouldn't be here." Jenny laid her cheek against his shoulder. "I wouldn't be dreading the day I have to go home and not see you every day."

"Don't dread that. It's not something that has to happen." He kissed the tip of her nose again. "Let me know when you're ready to go home and I'll spend time with you there... or you're welcome to come home with me too." He hadn't planned to make that offer, but now that it was out, he couldn't regret it. He'd not had anyone over to his place since he'd been back, hell, he hadn't been in it more than a few weeks. It was barely more than a few empty rooms. But if she wanted to see it, he'd love having here there.

Her eyes went wide. "Really?"

"Really, sweetheart." In fact, the more Snake thought about it, the more he realized, he didn't want to go back there without her. But how could he admit that, even to her?

40

J enny couldn't think of anywhere she wanted to be more right now than right here in Snake's arms, her head resting on his shoulder. Well, it might be better if they were up in her bed, naked. But she really didn't mind where they were. And it would be nice if she didn't have the cast that was still hardening on her leg. But the cast would be better than the brace and eventually, it would go away too.

She closed her eyes and took a deep breath, letting the now familiar sweat, leather, and motor oil scents she'd learned to associate with Snake, the yeasty scent of beer she'd come to associate with the clubhouse, even the musky scent of Chuy's cologne. The warmth of her man at her back, his arms wrapped around her middle calmed her.

Small sounds told her Kinard was back and busy packing up the case he'd set beside the table, but she didn't open her eyes. She hoped the small thing would keep Chuy from coming back and grilling the two of them, at least until the medic declared the cast now encasing the bottom half of her left leg complete and she could get up and get away from her brother when he pissed her off. And she had little doubt he would. The real question was if he would let her get away or if he'd chase her down to have his say.

"Let's take a look here." Kinard's voice warned her before she felt the gentle pressure of his hands on her cast, not that she could feel it through the cast, but she opened her eyes to find him repositioning her leg. That was what she'd felt. He seemed to be pressing several spots up and down her leg before laying it down on the chair, much as it had been before he'd gotten started. "All set. It looks good. Remember, keep it dry and –"

"And no weight on it," Snake finished for him, making Jenny smile. "We heard you last time and I haven't forgotten in the last ten minutes."

"Good. If you have any questions or problems, call me, or if you can't get a hold of me, Deanna can help too." He picked up the case that was now closed and fastened, then left, nodding to some of the other men on his way.

"Deanna?" Jenny asked.

"His woman. She's a nurse too."

Snake's voice next to her ear made her want to take him upstairs and insist he put his hands on her. Well, more of her than they were on now. More than they could be on while down here.

"Now that he's gone, we need to talk," Chuy's voice was hard and determined.

She opened her eyes to find him standing on the other side of the table, hands on his hips as he scowled down at her and Snake.

"Dude. You're harshing my mellow," she heard herself saying it before she'd planned it, then felt Snake's shoulder shake with laughter as she looked up at the confusion on her brother's face and fought to keep hers straight.

"Where the hell did that come from and did Kinard give you something? Are you high?" He looked at her like she'd lost her mind, then his gaze flicked to Snake for an explanation. "Do you know what the hell she's talking about?"

"Bro," Snake's voice held barely restrained laughter, "she's not high, she hasn't had anything but Tylenol or ibuprofen for a couple days."

"Then what the hell is she talking about?"

"It's a movie quote. She's spent a lot of time in the last week with only the TV for company and while we've got cable, sometimes the only thing worth watching is old movies. His chest still vibrated with laughter, though his arms around her kept her secure against him.

"What is this all about? I thought you were going to tone it down, at least in front of me." Chuy motioned to the two of them, a scowl still marring his brow.

"I'm not talking to you as long as you stand there like some avenging angel. I already told you you're harshing my mellow."

"What the hell do you mean by that?" he demanded again.

"She means she's relaxed and you're stressing her out," Snake translated. He used a foot to push the chair Kinard had been sitting in away from the table. "Sit down and be civil if you want to talk to us. Otherwise, I'll take her back upstairs and lock the door, so you have to leave us alone."

"The hell you will!" Chuy's indignant tone battled with his manner as he pulled out the chair and sat.

"Calm the hell down. I know it's a shock to come home and find everything that's happened, but everyone is okay, or will be soon. No one was forced to do anything against their will."

Jenny spoke up then, "We've been over this already. I told you I'm not going to go over again that these guys did what I asked them to by not telling you how bad I was. I'm glad they did. As for me and Snake? We could lay it at your feet. You are the one who paired me with him for the wedding. Speaking of which, I wish you could have stayed for your whole honeymoon though. When can I see Jill?"

Chuy blinked, as if it took him a moment to process everything she'd said.

"Any reason for not wanting to be here other than your fierce independence?" he asked.

"Not really. I thought I could get by on my own." She lifted one shoulder and let it drop, not bothering to pick her head up from where she still lay against Snake.

Her brother's gaze flicked back between her and the man sitting behind her for a moment then he pinned her with a look that clearly said he would know if she was lying. "And this is what you want? Him?"

"He is." She didn't hesitate.

"Even if he gets surly and acts like an asshole sometimes?"

"Don't we all sometimes? Hell, look at you now." She paused to let her eyes skim down him and back up, just to make a point. "But yes. Snake is what I want. I don't think that will change, but if it does, I'll let you know."

Chuy watched the two of them silently for a moment then shook his head. "I can't say I like it. He's not good enough for you. But then I probably won't think anyone is. I'll get used to it, as long as he treats you right." He shot Snake another scowl as he stood. "Take care of her and I won't have to beat your ass." He moved around the table, careful not to bump the chair her foot still rested on and stepped up beside her. "Take care, sis, and feel better. I'll bring Jill by to see you soon. Maybe tonight if she feels up to it." He bent and kissed the top of her head then stepped back. "Call me if you need anything."

"We won't." Snake spoke up behind her. "You take care of your woman. I'll take care of mine."

Chuy scowled at Snake then met her gaze, waiting until she nodded her agreement then turned and left. She hoped he was going back to Jill. They still had one day left on their honeymoon, and even if they were home, they should spend it together.

"What's this about your woman?" she asked once her brother was gone. It wasn't that she didn't like him calling her his, but sometimes a woman wanted to be asked. "I didn't agree to anything like that."

"Sure, you did, sweetheart."

He seemed content to sit just like this. That was okay with her, she was comfortable and liked having his arms around her, and she didn't care that they were in the middle of the clubhouse where anyone who walked in could see them. It wasn't like they'd spent time much of anywhere else in the last week.

"When?"

"When you asked me to your bed. You're not some piece of ass to be played with and we all knew it. I wouldn't have climbed in there with you unless I was serious about you."

"And you are? Serious I mean?" Her heart seemed to thunder in her ears. She'd only recently realized how much he meant to her. She hadn't dared to hope he felt something too. But did he?

"Sweetheart, you're mine. I'm not sure I could walk away if I wanted to." His arms tightened around her middle for a brief moment then relaxed.

"What if I wanted you to?" she asked, her voice barely more than a whisper.

"I'd try to convince you otherwise. I'd try to figure out how I screwed up and how to fix it. I don't know, but I wouldn't keep you against your will. I hope you know that. I love you for who you are, sweetheart, and keeping you if you want to go would kill that." He fell silent for a couple of seconds then spoke again, his voice barely more than a whisper against her ear, "Are you asking me to let you go?" His arms went rigid around her, but didn't tighten, as if all of a sudden, his whole body was filled with tension.

Her throat seemed to close as emotion overwhelmed her. She couldn't force the words past the knot there. Instead, she shook her head.

"Thank God," he breathed against her neck as he relaxed once more. "What do you want to do today?"

"Take me home."

"Home?"

"My place, your place, I don't care which, but I want us somewhere other than here, in a space where I don't feel like everything we say or do is public knowledge."

"Why?"

"Because I want to show you how I feel, and I don't want to have to bite my lip to keep from screaming when I finish or worry about who might hear us and what they might say to my brother."

"Jesus, sweetheart." He dropped his head until his chin rested on her shoulder. "You're going to be the death of me. I can tell already."

"Yeah? But think what a ride it will be."

"I already know. It might get a little rough, but life with you will be one hell of a ride." He helped her to her feet, handed her the crutches and moved to stand a couple of feet away. "Is there anything you need from upstairs before we head out? I need to run up and get the truck keys."

"Just my house keys, if that's where we're headed."

"I'll grab them." He took off moving fast. She watched him climb the stairs, unable to keep the grin off her face at her plan to get him in her bed and show him just how much she loved him. Especially now that she knew he loved her too.

It wasn't where she'd planned to be, but things worked out for the best. She couldn't imagine a better guy than the one she'd landed. Well, maybe her brother, but ewww. And she'd have killed him in short order.

No.

It was better that it was Snake. He'd snuck in and stolen her heart and she didn't even want it back.

Thank you for reading Snake, part of the Demented Souls series series. Please consider leaving a review on your favorite retailer.

If you're looking for more from Melissa Stevens please consider joining her VIP reader list for weekly updates on what she's working on now, as well as specials, giveaways and more.

All of her works can be found on her website at http://melis sastevens.us

Milton Keynes UK
Ingram Content Group UK Ltd.
UKHW010631040424
440620UK00001B/27

9 798224 234295